HAUNTED
LIVERPOOL

VOLUME FIVE

Published by The Bluecoat Press, Liverpool
Book design by March Graphic Design Studio, Liverpool
Cover illustration by Tim Webster
Printed by Grafo

ISBN 9781904438755

THE BLUECOAT PRESS
3 Brick Street
Liverpool L1 0BL

Telephone 0151 707 2390
Website www.bluecoatpress.co.uk

Front cover *A Soldier's Return*, page 85

TOM SLEMEN

HAUNTED LIVERPOOL

VOLUME FIVE

THE BLUECOAT PRESS

CONTENTS

INTRODUCTION

In this book I have collected together another selection of tantalising local mysteries and hauntings, many of which remain unresolved; such mysteries as the Lion Boy of Jubilee Drive – an unfortunate child born with a head of hair encircling his face like a lion's mane. His facial features were also rather unusual and added to the effect. Many people from Kensington have written to me about the Lion Boy over the years, and several of them stated that the child was mentioned in the Liverpool Echo in the early twentieth century. To date, I have not managed to trace him, but I'll keep delving, of course, because my curiosity in such matters is never satisfied.

Another conundrum that has never been satisfactorily answered, is contained in an intriguing comment made by John Lennon on the evening of Wednesday, 11 April 1962. John had recently arrived in Germany to see his friend and former Beatle, Stu Sutcliffe, only to discover that he had just died from a brain haemorrhage. Before the performance, John went on stage and made an announcement: "Stuart Sutcliffe was a very special human being and a remarkable man. He once told me that he had the ability to see into the future, and I for one now believe that Stu was telling the truth." What had happened to cause Lennon to say this? We will probably never know and it continues to vex Beatle biographers to this day.

Whenever I think of the human need to solve a puzzle, I muse on a riddle once posed by Lewis Carroll, the Cheshire-born author of the delightfully surreal *Alice in Wonderland* books. "Why is a writing desk like a raven?" asked the Mad Hatter, who attends the tea party with Alice, the March Hare and the Dormouse.

"Have you guessed the riddle yet?" the Hatter says, turning to Alice.

"No," says Alice, "I give it up. What is the answer?"

"I haven't the slightest idea," the Hatter tells her.

Readers of the book, however, chose to try and solve the riddle, even though the Mad Hatter suggests that there is no real answer. They pondered on the question certain that Carroll had posed it deliberately, knowing that there was an actual answer if you thought long enough. I remember my English teacher at school mentioning the raven and writing desk puzzle. He was just telling us that no one had ever solved it, when a man painting the outside of the school pushed open the window and said, "I know the answer".

"Really?" said the teacher, with a faint air of condescension.

"Edgar Allan Poe. Poe wrote on them both," said the painter. "He wrote a poem called *The Raven* and he must have written it on a writing desk. So that's the connection between a raven and a writing desk."

"Hmmm, I see ... but I doubt it though," said the teacher, sounding like the pompous Captain Mainwaring character out of the *Dad's Army* television series. The cultured painter sulkily closed the classroom window and resumed his task. Everyone in the class then attempted to solve Carroll's puzzle, but no one came up with anything remotely convincing. People will always attempt to solve the riddle, because we all have this inborn need to know things that are unknown. The comedian Dave Allen once remarked how people sometimes watch a ringing telephone for ages, unwilling to answer it because they don't want to speak to anybody, and as soon as the ringing stops, they say, "I wonder who it was?"

It was curiosity that spurred us to land on the moon, and to discover America, and it is that same inquisitiveness which causes a baby to touch a flame. Inquisitiveness sparked the young Albert Einstein to wonder about the speed of light, and what it would be like to ride on a light beam. I myself have often wondered just why light travels at the speed of 186,281 miles per second. Why that specific six-figured velocity? Through the exploration of such innocent questions, entire orthodoxies of thought have been toppled.

In May 1954, at the age of twenty-five, Roger Bannister ran a mile in under four minutes. It took him three minutes and fifty-nine seconds. Bannister had broken a psychological barrier that had existed since the days of Ancient Greece; something which many physicians and sportsmen had stated was an impossibility. As soon as Bannister broke through the barrier, others followed closely on his heels. Only forty-six days later, Australian John Landy lowered the record to three minutes and fifty-eight seconds. By 1979, Sebastian Coe had shaved nine seconds off the record, and by the fiftieth anniversary of Bannister's record, over nine hundred and fifty-five men had run a mile in under four minutes.

In 1994 a forty-one-year old man named Eamonn Coghlan beat Bannister's record, and by 2001 Hicham El Guerrouj brought the record down to three minutes and forty-three seconds. I wonder how long it will be before the three-minute mile becomes a reality, and if there will ever be an ultimate limit to the speed a human can achieve on two legs.

The tales that follow on the pages of this book may leave you asking healthy questions on the nature of life, death, time and space, and our place in the Cosmos. Even the comparatively minor local mysteries I have documented, 'pygmies of triviality' as Sherlock Holmes might call them, might reanimate the childhood sense of magical curiosity that is sadly jaded in so many adults.

Tom Slemen

THE TEACHER CLOCK

I first heard of the strange case of the Teacher Clock from my grandmother when I was a child, and have researched it over the years to glean the following details.

In Edwardian times, Herbert A Strong, a Professor of Latin, lived in one of the grand old houses in Liverpool's Falkner Square. He was a stern and highly studious academic with a formidable temper. His own children had grown up and flown the nest, but in the summer months, the professor's eight-year-old niece, Jesamine Middleton, often travelled from her home in Childer Thornton to stay at the house. Unlike Professor Strong's servants, who lived in constant fear of their master's mood swings and fiery temper, the pretty little red-haired girl adored her Uncle Herbert, and he had a soft spot for her, although he was usually far too haughty to show his affection openly.

Despite having received an excellent education, Jesamine still had great difficulty reading and speaking certain words, and probably had some form of dyslexia. She said things like 'chimley' instead of chimney, and 'donimo' instead of domino, and had great difficulty remembering and reciting the alphabet in its proper order. The children at school cruelly nicknamed her 'Muddled-up Middleton' and 'Mixed-up Jesamine' and she became increasingly anxious and did not want to go to school.

Aware of Jesamine's difficulties, Herbert attempted to give her intensive private lessons in spoken and written English, but his strong-arm approach only served to make her too nervous to learn. He would slam the chalkboard duster down on the desk and shriek, "Chimney! For Mercy's sake! Say it, child!"

"Ch ch chim...er...ley," Jesamine would stammer, her face bowed. Sometimes she would burst into tears and hide inside her aunt's wardrobe, where she would crouch down amongst her aunt's lavender-smelling finery, with all the hated jumble of letters and difficult words jangling round inside her head.

One afternoon, just after she had arrived at her uncle's house and handed her coat to one of the servants, Jesamine was surprised to notice an unfamiliar grandfather clock towering above her in the hallway. The moment she set eyes upon it, the clock began to chime melodiously, and Jesamine smiled in response. The clock was made of the finest mahogany, with beautiful marquetry panels, and had a very elaborate gold face. She had never seen it before, or at least she had never noticed it.

Filled with curiosity, she opened the door on the front of the clock and watched, mesmerised, as the shining golden pendulum swung slowly to and fro. Her eyes moved from side to side, as they followed the long, heavy pendulum as it beat the time. The ticking sound seemed to echo round the oak-panelled hallway and as she listened, within the ticking there came a faint voice that spoke the letters of the alphabet, clearly and rhythmically. The voice was that of a softly-spoken woman, and it was very calming and reassuring to Jesamine. In the large, shiny, round weight at the bottom of the swinging pendulum, the face of a smiling old woman gradually appeared, yet the little girl wasn't in the least afraid. The woman's lips moved as she recited the alphabet in a lilting, sing-song voice.

Time seemed to cease while Jesamine stood, transfixed, before the old clock. When a servant came down the hall and gently asked her what she was doing, the hypnotic spell was instantly broken. Without thinking, Jesamine rushed into her uncle's study and recited the full alphabet, perfectly, without hesitation. Professor Strong was very impressed at his niece's sudden, and almost miraculous improvement. How had she managed to learn her alphabet in such a short space of time, after so many months of fruitless study? Jesamine mysteriously explained that the clock had taught her the alphabet. He gave her a puzzled look as she stood before him bristling with new-found confidence. For once, he managed to hold his tongue and instead praised his niece, which served to boost her confidence.

Throughout the remainder of that summer, Jesamine would often be found standing spellbound before the old clock, tracking the pendulum's swing with a look of utter fascination. At school she began to write impressive, well-written and seemingly well-researched tales of kings and battles, of Christopher Columbus and the Great Fire of London – all of which had been told to her by the 'Teacher Clock' as she insisted on calling it. Her grammar improved dramatically, as did her speech and diction, and when her taunting classmates asked Jesamine what her favourite game was, she would eloquently reply, "Dominoes, of course" and wait to see their reaction.

Though delighted by his niece's rapid and unexpected progress, Professor Strong felt unnerved by her tales of the Teacher Clock, and her seemingly trance-like behaviour as she stood before it. The clock had been left to him in an old friend's will: retired teacher, Mrs Denny. Had Mrs Denny's spirit somehow been incorporated into the fabric of the old clock? Was it possible that she had returned from beyond the grave to gently coach her last pupil, Jesamine Middleton?

THE FLYING NUN

The religious Order of Mercy was founded in Ireland on the banks of the River Liffey in 1831, and the Sisters of Mercy were soon doing their good work in many other parts of the world. One of their convents was built in England in Victorian times, in Liverpool's Mount Vernon Street. By the 1960s, the Mount Vernon Street Convent had closed, but by that time the building had acquired a supernatural reputation in the local community.

In the early 1960s, two youths from Hall Lane in Low Hill decided to burgle a house on Mount Vernon Street, facing the derelict convent. The house was inhabited by an old spinster who was known in the neighbourhood as Miss Smith. The youths had chosen their target deliberately – local gossip had it that she had all her life savings hidden in the house. Miss Smith was regarded as something of an eccentric because she had pictures of the Scared Heart and the Virgin Mary on display in most of her windows. Her front parlour was described by some of her more secularly-minded neighbours, as being like the Vatican, with ornate crucifixes on the walls and statues and relics of the saints and Jesus and Mary dotted about.

One foggy December evening at around nine o'clock, the two youths, seventeen-year-old Raffy (short for Raphael) and nineteen-year-old Teddy, watched the spinster's house from across the road. Behind them, in the fog, stood the crumbling, twelve foot high wall of the old convent. A dim light suddenly started to glimmer in the upstairs bedroom of Miss Smith's house, and after about five minutes, it went out. This was the signal they had been waiting for. Raffy scurried across the road and sidled down an alleyway which gave access to the back yard door of the spinster's house. The door was securely bolted, so Raffy quickly scaled the wall and lowered himself noiselessly down into the back yard. He then used nothing more sophisticated than a thin wooden stick from an ice-lolly to insert into a gap in the window frame to knock off the catch.

Whilst all this was going on, Raffy's accomplice, Teddy, was alarmed to see a middle-aged man on a push-bike approaching from the direction of nearby Minshull Street. Teddy quickly put a cigarette in his mouth and cupped his hands around it to partly shield his face. As the cyclist passed by he didn't even glance at Teddy, but instead, he looked up with alarm above where Teddy was standing in the shadow of the wall, at something behind him. With relief, Teddy watched the red light of the bicycle fade into the murky fog, then his attention was drawn back to the front door of Miss Smith's house across the road. It opened slowly to reveal Raffy, who stood there, silently beckoning Teddy. As Teddy was about to enter the spinster's house, Raffy pointed towards the high wall of the former convent across the road.

"Who's that?" he whispered nervously.

Just beyond the top of the wall was the head of a strange figure, which bobbed up and down several times. The two burglars stood uncomfortably in the hallway of the house, not quite sure what they should do next. Who was this strange witness spying on them from the old convent? Next, they saw the figure emerge as far as its waist over the wall, and it became clear that what they were seeing was a nun dressed in a white habit. The two youths had obviously surmised that the woman was standing on some type of platform, or step-ladder, behind that high wall – when she eerily rose right up over the wall until she was suspended in mid-air. After a moment or two hanging, suspended before their eyes, she started to fly through the air across the road towards Raffy and Teddy.

As you can imagine, the sight of the airborne nun zooming towards them sent the two criminals scrambling for cover. Abandoning all thoughts of continuing with the robbery, they rushed through the hall to the back of the house, intending to make an escape down the back alleyway – but when they scuttled out into the back yard, they were confronted by the sight of the ghostly nun standing on top of the back yard wall. Her pallid face seemed as white as her habit, and her sunken eyes were black and lifeless. At this point, someone let out a scream in the neighbouring yard, as if they too had seen the spooky nun standing on the wall. The youths turned on their heels and fled back through the house and left via the front door. They ran panting and screaming down Mount Vernon Street with the nun's livid white form hovering close behind them. When they finally reached their homes in Hall Lane, they were relieved to find that the apparition had vanished.

The two youths were convinced that the nun's appearance had not been a coincidence. Her behaviour had left them in no doubt that she wanted to thwart their plan to rob old Miss Smith. Not wishing to provoke a return visit from the ghostly nun, they never went anywhere near the old convent again.

Miss Smith is thought to have once been a nun herself in her younger years, but no one is quite sure. The identity of the flying nun of Mount Vernon Street remains a mystery, but local people have reported seeing her on many other occasions, floating over the convent wall.

DEAD MAN WALKING

To preserve confidential details, the names of the persons mentioned in the following story have been changed.

Arrad Street is an L-shaped back-street that runs from Hope Street to Oxford Street, passing behind a row of houses and the Everyman Theatre. Today it is a lonely, dimly-lit street, but in the 1950s it was even darker, with just a solitary lamp on Oxford Street to illuminate one end of the narrow, cobbled passageway. In the April of 1956, Arrad Street was the backdrop to a very uncanny event. Before I proceed, I must go back further in time to the autumn of 1955.

On a November evening of that year, there was an electrifying boxing match at Liverpool Stadium. Liverpool's own middleweight, Billy Ellaway, dazzled the crowds with his onslaught against Guyana-born Kit Pompey. In the audience, a man and a woman sat in their ringside seats, holding hands as they watched the journeymen pugilists engaged in combat. Archie MacIntyre, aged forty-five, and his twenty-one-year-old fiancée, Tina Carney, were rooting for Ellaway, and when the local boxer won the contest on points, the couple went to celebrate the victory at a local pub in St Paul's Square.

At this pub Archie was approached by a man who discreetly took him to one side, and then dropped a bombshell. He said that he had seen Tina with another man, leaving a Lime Street cinema on the previous Sunday. Archie, trying to remain calm, asked Tina for an explanation. Initially she denied that she'd been with another man, but Archie subsequently rummaged through her handbag and discovered a passionately penned love letter, addressed to Tina, and pinned to it was a photograph of an unknown young man.

She broke down and finally confessed to seeing Larry Thompson, from Cicero Terrace. She had met him at the Kempston Street factory where she worked, and had been seeing him secretly for about four months. To make matters worse, Tina had recently told Archie that she was pregnant and, as a result, he had obtained a huge loan from a moneylender to finance a lavish wedding. Now Archie's hopes and dreams lay in tatters, thanks to some punk named Thompson. Archie was renowned for his violent temper, and he swore to his older brother Frank that he would kill him for wrecking his relationship. Archie had many contacts in Liverpool's underworld, and soon managed to obtain a gun. Meanwhile, he kept Tina imprisoned inside a locked room in his home and dictated a letter she was forced to write to her secret lover.

With tears in her eyes, the broken-hearted girl wrote the letter and it was posted immediately. Larry received it the next day and read Tina's words. She wanted him to meet her at Arrad Street at the rear of the Hope Hall theatre on Tuesday night at half-past nine. At Archie's insistence, Tina wrote that she thought Archie was having her followed, and Arrad Street was the only place safe enough to meet.

Larry Thompson fell for it all, hook, line and sinker, and arrived at Arrad Street in his car. Archie lurked at the darker end of the street, wearing a pulled-down trilby and a dreary fawn gabardine suit. He watched the headlights of Thompson's car die shortly after the vehicle pulled up near the back of the theatre. Archie nervously felt for the cold metal of the pistol in his coat pocket as he waited.

Eventually, out of the gloom of Arrad Street, came the youthful figure of Larry Thompson. He looked exactly as he looked in the photograph which he'd found in Tina's possession. His rival in love seemed to walk rather unsteadily down the unlit street, until he was about ten feet away. Archie then withdrew the pistol from his coat pocket and aimed it at the figure. Larry threw up his arms defensively with a look of horror on his face, as he stared at the gunman. Archie fired the pistol three times – right at Larry's chest area. The bullets went straight through him and chipped the brickwork of the wall on the left side of the street. Larry clutched his chest and seemed to be in shock. Archie swiftly turned and ran across Hope Street, down Maryland Street, before nipping down South Hunter Street, where his car was parked in an unlit corner.

They say that the criminal always returns to the scene of his crime, and that's exactly what Archie did. After hurling the pistol into the River Mersey at the Pier Head, Archie motored around the night streets for a while, then drove up Oxford Street and slowed down as he passed Arrad Street. He could see Larry Thompson's car, still in the exact same spot where the dead man had parked it. There was no sign of a policeman, or any sort of activity and that baffled Archie.

When he arrived home he broke out into a cold sweat. He was a mess. His brother Frank told him not to worry, as he and five associates would swear in court that they had been playing poker with him at the time of the shooting. He reminded Archie that Tina had been warned that she'd be knifed if she opened her mouth. Archie steadily went to pieces. His hands started to shake uncontrollably and he kept on repeating that he should not have taken a man's life just because he had been betrayed in love. Archie even talked about going to the police station to turn himself in, but Frank reminded him that he'd hang if he did that, and he plied his trembling brother with several glasses of neat scotch to calm his nerves.

In the bedroom upstairs, Tina wailed, knowing that a terrible revenge had been exacted upon her lover. Frank and Archie sat up all that night expecting a heavy knock at the door, but none came. Every page of the *Liverpool Echo* and other newspapers was scanned by the two men the next day, but there was no mention of the murder. Archie insisted that he had blasted Thompson in the chest. It was highly unlikely that anyone could have survived a shot in the chest at such close range. Archie even remembered seeing the bullets hit the wall behind Larry, so they could not have been blanks.

That evening, Archie and Frank discovered to their horror that Tina had somehow managed to escape from the room upstairs by climbing out of the window on to a shed in the back yard. The girl dashed to the nearest police station and within minutes, detectives and constables were paying Archie and Frank a visit. The two brothers had no alternative but to open the door to them. The men were quizzed at the police station, and a detective asked Archie why he had kept Tina confined against her will in the bedroom. Archie assumed that Tina had also told the police how she had been forced to write Larry Thompson a letter, luring him to the ambush in Arrad Street. He also presumed that the man's body had been found, so he blurted out his confession to the shooting. "It was a crime of passion," he said, with a tremor in his voice. "I shot Larry Thompson." The police looked at one another, baffled. Larry Thompson had not been shot. He was certainly dead, there was no question about that, but there was not a scratch on him. Naturally, Archie was confused on hearing this. The police said that Thompson had died from a rare heart condition called cardiomyopathy, which often affects young people. He had died in his car just after he had parked it in Arrad Street.

After issuing Archie with a warning never to go near Tina again, the detective angrily added that wasting police time was a serious offence, and he told him to beat it. The detective assumed that Archie had somehow learned of Larry's death, and had then subjected Tina to psychological torture by pretending that he had killed her lover. The letter Tina had written to Larry, asking him to come to Arrad Street was not dated, so the police disregarded it.

Archie later visited Arrad Street with his brother and showed him the three bullet marks in the wall, but there were no signs of any bullets. The brothers left the street, and just before they drove away, Frank broke the silence. He turned to his brother and said, "I wonder if you shot a ghost?" Archie was rather taken aback by the question. Frank hypothesised that perhaps when Larry had died of natural causes in the car, his ghost had left the vehicle in an effort to keep its appointment with Tina, and perhaps it was this apparition that Archie had shot. The bullets had indeed travelled through the ghost's chest and hit the wall behind it, but the ghost – being already dead – could not be killed. Archie had immediately turned and fled, assuming he'd killed a flesh and blood person. Archie remembered that Larry had reflexively thrown up his arms as he opened fire on him. Frank speculated that perhaps at that point Larry had not even realised that he was dead, and had therefore thrown his arms up in fright at the sight of the gun.

The MacIntyre brothers said a prayer for Larry at a church on the way home, and the strange incident caused them to undergo a change of heart which gradually led them to turn their backs on crime.

THE MAIDEN IN THE TOWER

I have written about timeslips before in my books, and the subject evidently fascinates my readers as much as it fascinates me, if the many emails and letters I receive are anything to go by. One of the most intriguing timeslip cases I have been researching is of a Liverpool man named Arthur Davies.

In the late 1930s, young unemployed people were strongly advised to sign up for a government training scheme designed to allow those who were out of work to go on to obtain employment. A propaganda film called *On the Way to Work* was widely shown to induce young people to give the scheme a try. The film featured idyllic rustic scenes of cloth-capped youngsters picking strawberries, making hay, chopping trees and damning streams.

One of the thousands of young men who were naïve enough to swallow the film's rather misleading view of country life was Arthur Davies, a twenty-year-old from Liverpool. Full of optimism, he signed off the dole and was taken to Presteigne in Mid-Wales, where he soon discovered the harsh reality behind the film's rosy promises. He'd become an inmate of what would later be known as a British Slave Camp, where unemployed people were 'reconditioned' to make them fit for the employment market. The taskmasters were ex-soldiers, who ran the camps with the strictest military discipline.

Arthur and the other recruits were awakened by a bugle call each morning at five. After the compulsory ritual salute to the Union Jack, they washed and shaved, consumed a meagre oatmeal breakfast, then took up a pick or shovel and worked for twelve hours. The weekly wage was just two shillings and a packet of Woodbine cigarettes. The labour camp Arthur was in was in a very remote part of Wales – the nearest pub was over twelve miles away – so he had little chance of enjoying his paltry wages.

Under the unbearable July sun, Arthur and the men of the camp were felling trees, hedging, ditching, and carrying out many other laborious tasks, when he noticed something glimmering from a nearby wood. At first he thought it was some mischievous local child reflecting the sun with a mirror to taunt the workers, and during his break, Arthur sneaked over to the wood, determined to catch the mischief-maker.

Upon entering a clearing, Arthur came across a magnificent sight, which left him wondering if he was dreaming. A huge stone castle stood on the far side of the woodland, on a rise. The turrets, battlements and drawbridge of the walled fortress were clearly visible above the treetops. Arthur turned to shout to a friend to come and join him, but he couldn't see anyone in the labour camp. He gazed back at the castle and couldn't resist walking through the wood to get a better view of the mysterious fortifications. A strange white flag fluttered above one of the towers, and far below, the still, green waters of the moat surrounded the castle walls.

A dazzling light suddenly flashed towards Arthur's, and it came from a figure leaning over a parapet on the castle keep. He squinted, and shielded his eyes with his hand. He could just distinguish that the figure was female, with long hair, and she seemed to be signalling to him with some kind of mirror. Arthur was suddenly overwhelmed with a deep feeling of sympathy towards the woman at the top of the tower, almost as if he knew her. He felt an urge to rescue her, and was ready to ascend the hill, when he heard voices behind him. He turned and saw two overseers from the camp advancing towards him. He didn't know what to do. He felt strongly drawn to the woman in the tower, but he knew that he would be in big trouble if he did not get back to work. Shirking, in any form, was not tolerated.

Arthur gazed back towards the castle in an agony of indecision – only to find that it was gone. The guards took hold of the youth, who had tears in his eyes, and escorted him back to the camp, giving him a severe warning about his behaviour as they did so.

Arthur told no one but his sister about the strange mirage, and for decades – right up until his death in 1972 – he regularly returned to that spot in Wales, in the hope of getting just one more glimpse of the elusive castle and the mysterious damsel who seemed to be a prisoner in its tower.

THE ANSWER BOX

In June 1963, Chris Keaton, a young lad from the Northwood area of Kirkby, went to stay with his Aunt Gladys on Netherfield Road in Everton for a week.

Aunt Gladys was a widow and always made a great fuss of her young nephew, as she had no children of her own. When he arrived, she told him to go and look in the wardrobe in her bedroom. There was something there for him.

Chris rushed into the room and mooched about for a while. He returned empty-handed with a puzzled look on his face. Gladys shook her head in dismay and went to look in the wardrobe herself. She immediately saw that Chris had accidentally pulled down her prized mink coat, which lay in a heap at the bottom of the wardrobe. She never wore it – it had been given to her by an old relative – but she loved the feel of its luxurious silky fur. She picked it up and said sarcastically, "It's under this old thing!" The sarcasm was totally lost on the boy; all he could think about was the surprise which his aunt had in store for him. With a nod and a wink, Gladys then pointed to an old hatbox at the bottom of the wardrobe.

"It's in there," she said. "Go on. Open it."

With a broad smile, Chris picked up the hatbox and opened it. Inside was a large black cowboy hat and a toy silver Colt Forty-Five gun – plus a box of caps. Within minutes, Chris had the hat on and was twirling the gun in his hand like a Western gunslinger. Gladys had to struggle not to laugh at the serious expression on her nephew's face. With an innocence that she found endearing, Chris asked if she knew that Kirkby was really called Dodge City, and he was the Kirkby Kid. Chris then challenged his own shadow to a draw, which was followed by a volley of caps. The cat scuttled behind the sofa, and cowered there until it was sure the noisy young intruder had gone out.

Chris was galloping his imaginary horse down Netherfield Road later that afternoon, still wearing his cowboy hat, when he saw someone that today's children would probably laugh at or ignore, but Chris's heart somersaulted. It was the ragman, pushing his old wooden cart, a limp yellow balloon trailing behind, shouting, "Rags! Any old Rags?" in a sing-song voice, which sent all the local children running excitedly into their houses and emerging shortly afterwards clutching handfuls of old clothes.

Chris remembered what his aunt had said about that old fur coat in the wardrobe – "this old thing", she had said. The boy turned and ran back home to fetch it. Maybe he could get a goldfish for his auntie in return. Aunt Gladys was at Mrs Prendegast's house enjoying her daily gossip. Chris grabbed the mink coat and made a beeline for the ragman, who quickly took it off his hands – a little too quickly. In return, Chris was given a purple party horn. He blew into it, and it unfurled a paper spiral that tapered to an orange feather.

"I want more than that!" Chris demanded, cheekily. "That there's me auntie's mink coat."

After a lot of grumbling, the ragman searched his pockets, then rummaged through the rags on his cart and eventually produced a small green plastic box which he handed to Chris.

"What is it?" the child asked.

"It's an Answer Box. Ask it any question and it will truthfully tell you the answer, but it can only answer yes or no."

Before Chris could ask any further questions, a voice echoing in the distance caught his attention. It was Aunt Gladys, and she wasn't happy.

"Christopher! Christopher! Come here at once. What have you done with my mink coat?"

Whenever an adult called him by his full name he knew it meant trouble and it stopped him in his tracks. By the time he had turned back again, the ragman's cart had trundled off down a side street and away, leaving a street full of children, each clutching a balloon, a whistle, or some other cheap toy.

Within seconds, Gladys had grabbed hold of Chris's collar and was marching him back home.

"That's it!" said Gladys. "You can stay in for the rest of the afternoon. I'm surprised at you, Christopher. I really am."

However, Gladys could not stay angry with him for long and after half an hour back at the house, they were chatting over a cup of tea. Chris decided that it would now be safe to show his aunt the box which the ragman had given him. Rather like Jack from the fairytale showing his mother the handful of beans he had received in exchange for her prize cow, Chris showed Gladys the Answer Box and told her it could answer any question.

"Oh! Pull the other one, you little rascal," said Gladys shaking her head. "I should box your ears, never mind playing with a silly plastic box."

Christopher, however, was unabashed. He was too busy examining the green box and particularly a little plunger button on the top. When he pressed it, the black pointer swung between the words 'Yes' and 'No'. Despite herself, Aunt Gladys seemed equally fascinated by the box, and she asked it, jokingly, "Will I marry a film star?" and then pressed the little button. A spring-loaded mechanism clicked, and the needle immediately swung to the word 'No'.

Chris giggled and he took hold of the box, "Will Auntie Gladys get married?" he asked, then pressed the button.

The box gave its unexpected answer: 'Yes'.

Gladys grinned. She'd lost her husband five years back, and had never really bothered seeing any man since. She did have an admirer, though – a man who lived across the road called Alan – although he was quite a few years younger than she was.

"Will the man I marry be called Alan?" she asked.

The box said, 'No'.

"Wonder who it will be, Auntie?" said Chris, and innocently quizzed the box with a series of further questions. "Will it be Father O'Hare?"

"Oh! Chris! You little monkey!" smiled Gladys, as the pointer on the box turned to 'No'.

"Will it be the coalman?"

'No.'

Gladys was pretending to treat the whole thing as a laugh, yet she was fascinated. Chris kept questioning the box, "Will it be the milkman?"

'No.'

"Will it be the clubman?" Gladys half-joked.

Chris repeated the question. "Will it be the clubman?"

'Yes,' came the answer from the box.

A big smile broke out on Chris's face.

Gladys was stunned.

"Auntie, you're going to marry the club man!" said Chris and, as an afterthought, he asked if she'd be having a big wedding cake. "You've got to have a big wedding cake, everybody does."

That week soon flew over, and Chris was back in his Kirkby home. He excitedly showed his dad the Answer Box, and told him about the dozens of answers it had already given. His dad laughed at first, but then he started to wonder as he gazed at the green box. He picked up the newspaper and turned to the racing section, and named each horse running in the 6.30 at Kempton, asking the box if it would win. When he reached a horse called Lovely Money, the box indicated 'Yes'. For every other runner it had read 'No'. Lester Pigott was riding on Lovely Money, which had odds of nine to two.

Chris's Dad couldn't resist giving the box a try. He put money on the horse and it won. "Was this just a coincidence?" he thought. The next horse – named Golden Plume – was also selected by the green box. It too won at odds of seven to one in the nine o'clock meeting at Kempton. And the next horse apparently chosen by the box also won.

Alan saw a change in his father which he didn't like. He wasn't content with his winnings, which were far more than he had ever won before. Instead, he wanted more and more. He talked about going through the pools coupon next, in an attempt to hit the jackpot. That night, when he was drunk, Chris's dad brought two friends around – Joey and Bobby – to show them the box. They laughed at his claims, but became deadly serious when he suddenly said, "Are you seeing another woman, Bobby?"

The box said 'Yes.'

Bobby went crimson and said, "Course I am – the missus."

Chris's dad could see his friend's discomfort but still

continued, "Is Bobby seeing another woman besides his wife?"

'Yes,' said the box.

This was true, Bobby was also seeing his neighbour's wife. To distract Chris's father, and without really knowing where the question came from, Bobby quickly asked, "Will Joey live to reach the age of fifty?"

The pointer quickly swung to 'No.'

"Will Bobby ever reach the age of fifty?" Chris's dad asked.

"Hey! Shut up, will you? I don't want to know," said Bobby, becoming increasingly nervous.

'No,' said the box.

Bobby and Joe were both aged forty-nine at the time. Bobby suddenly erupted and knocked the Answer Box out of Chris's hand and it hit the floor. Something cracked inside it.

"Look what you've done!" cried Chris. "That's my special box that the ragman gave me."

He picked up the box and it rattled. When he pressed the button, the needle refused to move. A fight broke out between Bobby and Chris's dad, and during the altercation, Joey picked the box up and threw it on to the back of the open coal fire. The green plastic soon melted, and as a series of green blobs dripped on to the burning coals, the inside of the box was revealed; nothing more magical than a few small springs and cogs.

A week before their fiftieth birthdays, Bobby and Joey died together in a car crash in Shrewsbury. Chris's Aunt Gladys did end up going out with the club man, and she married him two years later.

Chris believes that the ragman – who was never seen again in the neighbourhood – was actually the Devil.

Perhaps it was all pure coincidence, or the result of

Chris's faulty recollections of his childhood. However, to this day, Chris is adamant that the Answer Box which was given to him by the ragman, was able to accurately predict future events, as sinister as they may have been.

CUPID'S SHOT

This story and the following one – A Dangerous Experiment – are both derived from the *Liverpool Albion, The Times*, and several books on Edwardian experiments in anaesthesia. They both concern the misuse of chemicals in an attempt to procure those precious things which money cannot buy.

One of the closely-guarded secrets of the ages is a potion that can make a person fall in love. This is not an aphrodisiac (named after Aphrodite, the Greek goddess of sexual love and beauty) but a concoction used to cause lust or desire. If you want to make a person fall in love, you must forget oysters, powdered rhino horn, Spanish Fly, ginseng and zinc supplements, because those things merely create sexual desire. Love, as most people realise, is quite a separate thing altogether, and the ancients created their potions to engender love by extracting certain chemicals from the poppy plant – and also from the flower universally associated with love – the red rose.

Many years ago, in the late 1880s, there was a pharmacy on Lord Street that employed an eccentric chemist named Connel McConnicky. McConnicky had been a pharmacist in Dublin, but had been sacked for creating a variety of concoctions with dangerous side effects. One of his best-sellers was a green tonic called McConnicky's Old Thought Provoker, which was a mild hallucinogenic tonic. But by far the most requested under-the-counter product which

McConnicky made was his legendary 'love potion', which he called Cupid's Shot. It was almost prohibitively expensive, retailing at two guineas for a tiny red-tinted bottle of the product, which was to be taken orally. Only the very rich could afford the concoction.

One Spring morning in 1882, Robert Montague, a dishonest businessman from the Cotton Exchange, sidled into the chemist's and discreetly waited until the shop was devoid of customers, before whispering to McConnicky that a friend had recommended Cupid's Shot. He slipped the two golden guineas into the chemist's outstretched palm. McConnicky stooped and reached for the under-the-counter 'medicine'. The tiny red bottle was rapidly wrapped in soft tissue paper and Montague slipped it into his inside coat pocket. After the sale was made, McConnicky gave him the simple instructions: "Pour the entire contents into a beverage which the lady is about to drink, and her heart will open like a rose." McConnicky explained that if the lady had the slightest feeling towards him, she would soon be smothering him with love and affection.

Mr Montague tilted his bowler hat and bade the unscrupulous chemist good morning. He dashed to the old Adelphi Hotel on Ranelagh Place, where he had arranged to have morning coffee with a beautiful young woman named Helena Yeoman. Helena was the nineteen-year-old daughter of Bernard Yeoman, a local entrepreneur who owned a vast empire of jewellery shops in Lancashire and Cheshire. Robert Montague had coldly calculated that if he were to wed Helena, he'd be marrying into enormous wealth. He didn't have any feelings for the girl, but looked upon her solely as an unprecedented business opportunity. Robert had managed to coax Helena into meeting him at the Adelphi hotel, where he was currently staying.

Helena sat in the lounge; a portrait of youthful beauty, and a waitress named Juliette stood nearby, paying her an unusual amount of attention, because she also knew who Helena Yeoman's father was, having once worked at Helena's Aigburth home for two years as a maid.

Robert bowed low and ostentatiously kissed the girl's knuckle. As he sat down at the table, he was apologising profusely because he was several minutes late. Helena forgave him and said that she had been enjoying a conversation with Juliette, the waitress. Coffee was ordered, and Juliette quickly brought it to the table. Robert was making polite conversation, when all of a sudden, a tall, handsome man in a top hat and the finest clothes, entered the lounge. He called Helena's name at the top of his voice and brushed past Robert, who was several years his senior, to embrace her.

The man was Eustace Buncey, an accomplished all-rounder in the sporting world, as well as being one of the most eligible bachelors of his day. Eustace spent a good half-hour at the table in the lounge, paying compliments to the lovely Helena, before finally taking his leave. Robert Montague seethed with envy and resentment as Buncey bragged about several estates he owned in South Africa that had been bequeathed to him by his late uncle.

Rid of the dashing young braggart at last, Robert Montague wondered how he could accomplish the task of emptying the little red bottle into Helena's coffee without her noticing. Even if he did manage to drug the coffee, she might not drink it. It was an expensive risk he had to take. Perhaps he should ask her to close her eyes, and pretend he had a surprise for her, and use the opportunity to pour the potion into the coffee.

As Robert Montague was still working out how to slip the drug into Helena's drink, she left the table after asking to be excused – to powder her nose. Juliette, the waitress, escorted her to the ladies' powder room. Robert looked shiftily about, reached into his pocket, then lurched forward and poured the contents of the red bottle into Helena's cup. He waited patiently for her return, trying not to show his impatience.

Helena eventually made her reappearance, and she immediately smiled at Robert, then began to take delicate sips of the coffee. Juliette stood a few steps behind Robert, waiting upon the couple. The minutes rolled by as Robert Montague steered his conversation from flat anecdotes about his colleagues at the Cotton Exchange, to the depth and unusual blueness of Helena's eyes. Those eyes suddenly looked heavily glazed. She started to breathe deeply, and she placed her hands over her bosom and smiled. It was a loving smile. She reached out towards Robert, and he reached back to her, but Helena roughly brushed his hands aside. Instead, she got up and headed straight for the waitress, Juliette, who was astonished by the sudden attention, yet smiling. The couple embraced and kissed one another passionately. The *Liverpool Albion* describes this, at the time, outrageous display of affection as a 'mania' brought on by the drug.

The red-faced Robert Montague protested meekly, but to no avail – the two women were inseparable from that moment and barely listened to his protestations. After several moments the embarrassed businessman meekly left the hotel, and fearing prosecution for administering the Cupid's Shot drug, boarded a train to Birmingham, where he laid low for a while.

Strange rumours spread that Helena and Juliette underwent a secret type of marriage service soon afterwards. They certainly lived happily together for seventeen years in North Wales. And Robert Montague had to look elsewhere to make his fortune.

A DANGEROUS EXPERIMENT

This story also concerns the misuse of a drug for selfish gain. In this case, it was not the abuse of a potion to kindle love, but over-indulgence in a dangerous mind-expanding drink that caused two egotistical men to become gibbering idiots.

The scene for this parable is Rodney Street, in Edwardian Times. In this Liverpudlian equivalent of Harley Street, at Number 78, was the practice of George Arthur Williams, a Harvard-educated dental surgeon. He was a man who also had a wide knowledge of anaesthesia. Williams had a cousin in Mexico who collected various plants with medicinal properties and dispatched them to him. Williams wrote several tracts on the coca plant from which the drug cocaine is derived.

In 1886, John Pemberton had introduced the popular drink Coca-Cola to consumers in America. Amongst other ingredients, the drink contained cocaine, syrup and caffeine. In 1901, the cocaine was removed from the soft drink, because it was thought to be addiction-forming. As far back as 3000 BC, coca chewing was practised throughout South America to stave off hunger and give extra energy, and the plant was regarded as a gift from God. The Incas cultivated large coca plantations that were later taken over by the Spanish invaders.

George Arthur Williams researched other less-known plants of medicinal value, such as the peyote cactus, which contains a chemical that transforms sounds entering the ear into a kaleidoscope of colours in the brain. Williams experimented with the cactus extract, but found it was of little use in the annulment of pain from tooth nerves. He also dabbled with Huanta, a toxic plant from Ecuador with white blossoms, which is reputed to be the main ingredient in the so-called 'Sorcerer's Drink' which caused shamans to fall into a coma for three days at a time, until they awakened imbued with supernatural wisdom. When Williams drank the diluted juice of the plant, he ended up with nothing more than a lingering headache.

However, the one plant that did seem to hold great potential for the creation of a new pain-killing compound, was a tropical American vine called Yage (pronounced ya-hay). This plant had acquired something of a legendary status in Europe, but obtaining it was exceedingly difficult, as it was mainly found in Amazonia. Williams received a parcel one morning from his cousin across the Atlantic. It was a coil of Yage vine measuring just thirty-six inches in length, sent from Belem in South America. Williams took down a huge, leather-bound volume on the exotic flora of the South American Continent and flipped through the pages until he came upon the section that documented the Yage plant and its use in various controversial preparations.

In order to extract the vital ingredient of the plant, a portion of the vine was to be boiled in distilled water for fourteen hours until it was reduced to a residue. The residue had to be further treated until its essence had been isolated. This distilled spirit then had to be rediluted by infusing it into wine made from the noha grape. The noha grape was banned in France in the 1970s by the French Ministry of Agriculture because the wine it produces is thought to cause insanity through the release of a chemical similar to an hallucinogen found in marijuana.

After several months, two bottles of the Yage wine were produced by Williams and stored in the cellars of 78 Rodney Street. Meanwhile, he devoured as much information on Yage as possible, and even travelled to the reading rooms of the British Library in London to read up on the plant, which was classified under the Latin name of *banisteriopsis caapi*. Williams read various accounts of the effects which Yage wine had on a person once it had been imbibed. Most people who had drunk the wine afterwards told how they had been confronted by terrifying, realistic monsters which did not seem to be Yage-induced hallucinations at all. Had they been drug-induced figments of the mind, the appearance and behaviour of the horrifying phantasms should have varied from person to person, but this was not the case. The people who perceived the monsters always described them in exactly the same way.

There were three species of these monsters: grotesque, gargoyle-like beings; globular black octopuses with squirming tentacles; and an enormous black cat, reminiscent of a panther. The Ecuadorian shamans maintained that these creatures could only be repelled by strong willpower. A weak-minded person would be attacked by them, and would either die, or return to the real world with an insane mind. Once the creatures had been tamed, the person who had absorbed the Yage wine would be capable of receiving 'cosmic wisdom' and communicating with the dead. The most hazardous part of the entire experiment hinged on consuming exactly the right quantity of wine. Too much, and it would result in incurable madness.

George Arthur Williams wrestled with the pros and cons of personally experimenting with the dangerous brew, and many times he took one of the unlabelled dark purple bottles of Yage wine from the cool cellar and gazed at it. He would repeatedly touch the cork and feel an almost overpowering urge to reach for the corkscrew. But he wasn't ready yet. What if the stories of the monsters from another reality were true?

At a gentlemen's club in Liverpool in May 1906, Williams was smoking his pipe as he stared out of the window into the evening sky. He was contemplating the possibility of using a guinea pig upon which to test the potent wine, when two acquaintances approached him and disturbed his reverie. They were the tall, broad-shouldered Saxon Hill, a successful stockbroker from St Michael's-in-the-Hamlet, and his friend Thomas Canning, a wealthy confectioner who had sold numerous cake recipe books to hotels across Europe. Williams talked to them about the dangerous wine, and the two men responded with sceptical smirks.

Saxon Hill bragged that he was immune to intoxication, and told a rambling story of how he had remained standing after a drinking spree that lasted twelve hours. Each of his other drinking companions finished up lying prostrate on the floor, and one drinker had almost died of alcohol poisoning.

Canning declared that he had never heard of Williams' Yage wine, despite the fact that he was one of the greatest wine connoisseurs in England. Hill lit a huge, ostentatious Havana cigar and offered himself as the ideal guinea pig the American dentist was looking for. Williams instantly took up his offer, but only on the condition that he would not be sued if the wine 'tilted' Hill's brain. Hill promised that he would get a solicitor to draw up a legal document that would exculpate Williams from any responsibility, should the wine incur any damage to his mental health. The stockbroker seemed excited at the possibility of trying the mystical wine, but Canning predicted that the proposed experiment would come to nothing. The confectioner said that he had once inhaled nitrous oxide in his youth because a medical student friend had sworn that the gas provided instant enlightenment. All it had done was make Canning giggle and feel as if he was caught between waking and sleeping.

On the evening of Monday 7 May 1906, Saxon Hill and Thomas Canning arrived together at 78 Rodney Street, and were admitted by a servant and shown into the drawing room, where a bottle of purple Yage wine stood in the centre of a small mahogany table on a silver salver. Next to the bottle was a crystal wine glass and a corkscrew fashioned from a piece of horn. Williams entered the room, and a smiling Saxon Hill handed him the legal document which guaranteed that no action would be taken against him, should the experiment end tragically. As Williams perused the document, Canning drew Hill's attention to an upright wooden chair which was swathed in thick leather straps. Williams explained that Hill would be put in that chair and restrained, in case he became violently hysterical as a reaction to the Yage. Most people in their right minds would have fled on seeing the chair, but the indomitable Hill seemed to be relishing the drama of the situation.

Saxon Hill inserted the corkscrew into the bottle as Williams warned him to be very careful. Williams began to have serious doubts about the experiment, not for Hill's sake, but for his own reputation. If the wine produced no effect, the American would be ridiculed for ever more. He was still wondering whether it was wise to proceed, when, all of a sudden, he felt a sharp nagging pain in his abdomen. The pain was so severe it winded him and made him double up. He had suffered from the same stomach pains at breakfast, and he feared it might be the return of what the doctors had diagnosed as a rumbling appendicitis. The pain receded for a while, and Williams sat at the table, breathing deeply, with his hand over his navel. Saxon Hill poured the wine into a glass, held it up to the bright gas mantle, then sniffed it. "Smells quite sweet," he said.

"Just sip it, Mr Hill," cautioned Williams.

But the foolhardy Hill ostentatiously threw back his head and downed the entire glass.

"No!" wailed Williams, all the time thinking about all the

literature he had read which warned about the dosage of the Yage and noha grape concoction.

"I say, calm down, man," said Hill, licking his lips. "The drink hasn't been invented which can damage my iron constitution!"

Williams took out his fob watch and removed the cover to inspect the dial. The time was 7.35pm. According to all the literature he had read, Yage took ten minutes to enter the bloodstream via the stomach wall.

As those ten minutes elapsed, Saxon Hill repeatedly announced that he felt as right as rain, and expressed disappointment with Williams who had promised such great things of the drink. At this point, having watched Hill down the wine with no obvious ill effects, Canning's curiosity got the better of him and he picked up the bottle, sniffed it's mouth, then took a small swig from it, even though Williams protested. "It tastes rather plummy," was his verdict, as he strode over to the window and gazed out at the gathering twilight.

Saxon Hill mentioned that he and his sweetheart Leonora would be travelling to New York on the White Star liner *Adriatic* on the following day, producing an expensive diamond ring from his waistcoat pocket, he told Canning how he planned to propose to her on deck in the mid-Atlantic.

"You romantic fool, Saxon," laughed Canning, and the confectioner turned – to find Saxon Hill trembling all over his body. He seemed to be having some kind of fit. His eyes bulged alarmingly, and he wore an expression of sheer terror on his contorted face. Williams noted Saxon's behaviour with a mixture of dread and curiosity.

"Saxon, what on earth's the matter, dear fellow?" asked Canning, going to the aid of his friend, but as he walked around the table he suddenly felt an intense, burning pain in the middle of his forehead, which forced his eyes to close tightly. Canning held his head in his hands and let out a horrible scream.

Saxon Hill was still standing, albeit with a rigid posture, despite the shuddering tremors which had gripped his body. He tried to utter something, but instead he began to foam at the mouth. His eyes seemed much whiter than normal and threatened to bulge out of their sockets. The foam frothed and dribbled down Hill's beard and on to his waistcoat.

Canning, meanwhile, was now face-down on the hearth rug, convulsing uncontrollably, and yelping the words, "Stop! Stop!"

At this point, a maidservant who had heard the commotion, barged into the drawing room and witnessed the horrendous sight of the two men gripped by some kind of strange insanity. As the servant looked on, Saxon Hill stumbled backwards into a corner and shielded his eyes with the back of his hand. With his bare hands, Thomas Canning started grabbing glowing pieces of coal from the fire and began hurling them at something only he could see on the floor.

Williams told the maid to fetch a doctor at once, and she closed the door and ran downstairs. She left the front door ajar and dashed across the road to the house of a Doctor Hamilton and informed him of the shocking scene she had just witnessed. When Hamilton and the maid entered the drawing room, they saw only Williams, initially, lying on the floor in obvious agony, clutching at his abdomen. Then the doctor and the maid heard the muffled sounds of someone crying. They traced the sobbing to Hill and Canning, who were cowering together under the table in abject terror.

Williams was taken to the Royal Infirmary on Pembroke Place, where an emergency appendectomy was carried out on him. He made a full recovery, and subsequently learned of the chilling fate of Saxon Hill and Thomas Canning who were not so lucky. Hill was being kept under lock and key in a room at the house of his brother, where he did nothing but tremble in a corner and mutter to himself. He had been certified insane and his family had been told that there was no hope of being cured. His sweetheart Leonora had sailed to America without him, and after learning of his insanity, had deserted him. Those who listened to Hill's ramblings said that he spoke of a hideous black squid, with a single green eye, that continuously coiled it's tentacles about him.

Thomas Canning's insanity made him a danger to himself as well as others, and he had been confined to a Lancashire lunatic asylum. He also told of being tormented by a repulsive tentacled creature that resembled a giant brown octopus, and of a long black panther, the size of a horse, which had glowing red eyes. Both creatures stalked him day and night. Canning felt so persecuted by the horrific creatures that he gouged out one of his own eyes in an attempt to blind himself. He later died in Bedlam lunatic asylum.

Saxon Hill never recovered and faded into obscurity. Having destroyed the lives of two of his friends, not surprisingly, Williams abandoned his experiments with hallucinogens. Drug researchers do not currently understand how Yage affects perception, and the noha grape used in the wine mixture is still banned in most countries.

THE GHOSTLY HARPIST

In the 1920s, the large Randall family of Kirkdale were forced to leave their crumbling home by the authorities, and they were moved to a large Victorian house on Everton Brow, which they found just as draughty and damp as their condemned home. It would be just a temporary move until more suitable accommodation could be found, they were told.

The Randalls soon settled into their temporary home, but it wasn't long before they realised that, as well as being uncomfortable, the place was haunted. It all started one stormy evening as the family gathered around the fire in the parlour, listening to their old Irish grandfather, Doogan. Doogan was telling the family one of his amusing tales of his youth in Dublin, when a strange, musical sound seemed to descend through the fabric of the house. At first everyone thought it was just the wind whistling down the chimney, as it was a stormy night, but when the gales quietened down, everyone could clearly distinguish what the sound was. Someone was playing a harp somewhere in one of the upstairs rooms.

One of the Randalls, a fifty-year-old navvy named Michael, came clattering down the uncarpeted stairs from his bedroom into the parlour. He'd been awakened from his slumbers by the eerie music, and had come to tell the rest of the family.

"We've heard it as well, Michael," said the Grandfather Doogan, and he added, "I don't like it at all. It's weird."

The grandaughters trembled and said, "What do you mean, Grandad?"

Before he could answer, everyone jumped and the women shrieked as the corner of the table-cloth suddenly lifted. But it was only little Danny Randall, eleven years of age. He'd been listening to his grandfather's comments about the strange music, so he was now frightened as well. He emerged from under the table where he'd been playing, and clumsily stepped on his grandfather's shoe as he lunged towards him.

"Get over here, Danny," said Danny's mother through clenched teeth.

The grandfather uttered the dreaded word – "Ghosts."

Danny's father puffed hard on his pipe and his four sons listened to the ghostly melody. What was the song being played? thought the older people present. Although it was very faint, and difficult to hear because of the wind, they all found it familiar. Then Danny's grandmother identified the song. It was an old favourite called *Irish Rover*. The music gradually drifted away until only the sounds of the crackling fire filled the uneasy silence. No one dared to climb the stairs to go to bed until three in the morning.

At breakfast the next morning, a cousin of the Randalls called at the house. His name was Gerald Mooney. He spent his life travelling all over England to find work, and was nicknamed the Irish Rover by both friends and family. Strangely, no one connected his visit to the song *Irish Rover* played by the ghostly harp the night before.

Once it was daylight, the sons of the Randall family and their cousin Gerald Mooney felt a little more courageous. Together, they climbed up into the garret, right at the top of the house under the eaves. The door into the garret was swollen and warped with damp and could only be opened with great difficulty. The young men all pushed together and the door finally swung open, shaking loose a pile of dust that had probably been undisturbed for years. As their eyes adjusted to the darkness in the dusty attic, they each made out the unmistakable form of a large harp. It was about five feet in height and stood upright in the centre of the room, festooned with cobwebs and thick dust. Wiping away some of the cobwebs, the sons soon found the words 'Dublin 1872' inscribed on the body of the harp's metal frame. Realising that it must be valuable, they brushed it down and tried to play it but it sounded out of tune.

The young men stepped back on to the landing, choking from the dust. As the Randall sons were discussing what they should do with the harp and, more importantly, how much they would get for it and who they could sell it to, they heard the instrument playing all by itself. The young men slowly turned … a red-haired woman dressed in a long green dress was sitting at the harp, plucking the strings to produce a beautiful, lilting melody. Her face was too pale for her to be living, and her dark eyes glared at the five men with pure contempt, as if they were trespassing into her domain. The young men fell over one another as they ran pell-mell out of the garret.

No one in the family dared to go back up to the garret after that terrifying encounter with the phantom harpist, and on some nights, the family would hear her playing various melodies. These titles of these melodies always seemed to predict something. The sombre strains of *Molly Malone* were plucked by the phantasm in the garret one night, and by the following morning, Mrs Randall was visited by her brother – who brought her the sad news that their sister Molly had died in her sleep during the night. Was this a coincidence, or had the harpist's choice of melody been a warning of the death? On another occasion, the harpist played the *Mendelssohn's Wedding March*, and this was the very evening on which one of the Randall sons chose to come home to tell his family that his young lady had just accepted his proposal for marriage.

But one night the sound of a melody made everyone apprehensive. It was unmistakably *Danny Boy*, a song that had been based on a very old melody called *Londonderry Air*. There was a line in the song which went, 'It's you, it's you must go.' Did this mean that Danny, the youngest in the family, was going to go away, or worse still – going to die? The strange thing was that Danny Randall loved the song, and often asked his grandfather to sing it to him.

That week, Danny rode a friend's rickety, homemade steering cart down the steep incline of Everton Brow, and he lost control of it and hit a brick wall, seriously injuring his head and his back. The boy was carefully carried into the house, and a doctor was sent for. By the time the doctor arrived, Danny was in a comatose state, and he said that, even if he was hospitalised, there was nothing that could be done to save him. Neurological know-how was very scant in those days and treatment for head injuries was very primitive, basically consisting of rest and quiet.

The family kept Danny at home, where fervent prayers were said for him and holy water was administered to his lips. The house which had always been filled with laughter and singing, was now awash with sadness. Everyone crept round on tiptoe and spoke in hushed whispers, as Danny hung on.

One stormy evening, as Danny's mother kept her vigil over her critically ill son, the family once again heard the ghostly strains of *Danny Boy* – the very same song that had seemed to foretell Danny's devastating accident. Suddenly, Danny's eyelids flickered, ever so slightly at first, then unmistakably – he was waking up! A miracle had happened! The next minute Danny opened his eyes fully as he finally woke up from his deathly coma. A faint smile was on his lips as he listened to his favourite song. To the delight of his family, Danny went on to make a full recovery.

A month or so later, shortly before the Randalls left the haunted house for good, *Chopin's Death March* was clearly heard coming from the old harp in the garret, and each member of the family looked around at the others without saying a word. Each knew exactly what the others were thinking – Who will die tonight? They were right; that night, old Grandfather Doogan passed away at the house.

For years, there were strange rumours that the red-haired phantom harpist was the troubled spirit of a girl who had been murdered at the house in the eighteenth century.

THE HANGED MAN

One pleasant evening in June 1960, seven sixteen-year-olds sat, squashed together on a park bench, in Edge Hill's Botanic Gardens, either side of a Kensington lad named Tommy Murphy – or Spud Murphy as he was known to other members of the gang, because of his fondness for chips. They seemed to be hanging on to his every word.

Seventeen-year-old Spud was reading out an article from the *Liverpool Echo* about a local lad who had been caught trying to rob Wavertree's Abbey Cinema. Police had inspected the premises after a tip-off, but had found no one. They were about to leave, when the police dog, Rinty, started barking furiously at the empty seats of the auditorium. A sheepish boy soon emerged from behind one of the seats and gave himself up.

Spud's gang laughed at the idea of being caught by a dog. Spud said there was easy money to be made in the robbing of a factory. One of the boys, Billy, said that Edmundson's Sweets factory, off Wellington Road, was supposed to have a safe that was packed with money. Billy had overheard his uncle – who had once worked at the factory – talking about it. What's more, the combination was kept on a piece of paper in a certain drawer of a filing cabinet in the same room. The factory's night-watchman was said to be a feeble old man. Even if the safe's contents couldn't be taken, Billy estimated that the sweet factory stock must be worth thousands, and they could help themselves! The rest of the gang all liked the idea and one of them suggested that they should carry coshes, but Spud Murphy silenced them all when he claimed that he could get hold of a pistol. That would be the only weapon they'd need.

Later that week, Spud and his ten-year-old brother waited in an alleyway near Gerard Gardens until they saw their Uncle Alfie leaving for his local pub, as he did every night. They knew that he would be there for the next two hours – plenty of time to break into his flat and find what they were looking for. Spud levered open the bathroom window of the flat and then helped his brother to squeeze through the window to open the front door of the flat. Spud knew that Uncle Alfie kept an old loaded First World War Webley revolver hidden in his bedroom, in case he was burgled.

As Alfie was enjoying his nightly pints of ale at his local, Spud was rummaging through every drawer and cupboard in his bedroom until he found what he was looking for under the bed, beside a chamber pot. He examined the pistol's chambers and found that they were loaded with six bullets. Spud gave his little brother a ten shilling note for his part in the robbery and told him that he had better keep his mouth shut about what had happened that night. He then set off for his girlfriend's house with the pistol stuffed in his inside pocket.

His girlfriend, Susan, was horrified when Spud showed her the loaded pistol, and she cried her eyes out when Spud told her about the planned robbery. "Don't be stupid, Spud," she cried. "You'll be hanged if you shoot anybody. It's not worth it. Throw that horrible thing away."

"No one's going to hang, and no one's going to get shot either!" Spud shouted at her.

At midnight, Spud and the seven members of his gang rendezvoused on Lawrence Road, then proceeded to the sweet factory on foot, in two groups of four. Most of them had never done anything worse than pinch a few penny sweets from the corner shop, and this was the first time any of them had been involved in anything as serious as this. They were all a bundle of nerves. Even Spud, for all his bravado, could feel his heart thumping in his chest, but he couldn't lose face now in front of the whole gang – they'd never listen to him again if he did.

As Spud and three others in his group were passing under the railway bridge that crosses Wellington Road, they came across a frightening sight. On the wall in front of them was projected the enormous shadow of someone hanging by the neck from a rope. They looked at each other, but said nothing. When the teenagers turned the corner they stopped in their tracks. A young man hung suspended from a girder of the railway bridge with a noose around his neck. His head was twisted at an unnatural angle and his eyes bulged in terror. His swollen, purple tongue protruded down past his chin, and from his throat came a hideous, bubbling, choking sound that chilled the would-be robbers to the bone.

Spud and the gang stood there under the swinging corpse, frozen in terror for a while, before fleeing in different directions. As Spud ran home, he told everybody he met about the hanged man. One or more of them must have dialled 999, because a police car and an ambulance rushed to the bridge within minutes. No hanged man, or any evidence of a hanging, such as a rope, or a noose, was found anywhere near the scene.

The ill-fated robbery was abandoned, and the next day Spud surreptitiously returned the revolver to his uncle's flat and he even helped him put his things back together, although he did not admit to him that he and his brother had actually perpetrated the break-in. From that day onwards, Spud went straight, as he believed that the vision of the hanged man had been some sort of supernatural omen, warning him that he would face the hangman if he shot anybody during the robbery. The rest of the gang all breathed a sigh of relief.

THE CASE OF THE
UNBORN DAUGHTER

In 1999, thirty-two-year-old Patrick from Aigburth, experienced a series of paranormal experiences that left him a changed man. They all began one Friday in the October of that year.

Patrick was unemployed and single, and he was leading a pretty aimless, depressing existence. On Fridays he usually dragged himself out of bed at around eleven in the morning, before setting off to cash his Girocheque at the Post Office. After collecting his money, he would call round to his friend Steve's house, and the two of them would then drive around aimlessly in Steve's car, without any particular purpose or destination in mind. They would just cruise around the neighbourhood, with Steve beeping the horn of his car at any women they found attractive. And Fridays were the highlight of Patrick's week!

On this particular Friday, Patrick and Steve went to the local pub, and proceeded to get thoroughly drunk on Patrick's Giro money. Several hours later they staggered to the local take-away to get themselves a kebab and some chips. On the way, they attempted to chat up two girls, who, like many others before them, rejected their drunken advances and stormed off in a huff. Steve then caught a taxi home, and Patrick walked unsteadily back to his flat, weaving drunkenly from one side of the pavement to the other. After finally managing to get his key into the keyhole in the front door, he let himself in.

Once inside, he flopped down on the sofa, which was littered with crumbs, newspapers and half-eaten chocolate bars, and drunkenly began to contemplate his lonely, futile existence. His mood sank lower and lower, and he decided to switch on the television to try and rid his mind of his depressing thoughts. He was still so intoxicated that he couldn't figure out how to change channels and he sat there, befuddled, watching an Open University programme on BBC2 until two in the morning.

Just as he was thinking about going to bed, a little girl, aged about five or six, came skipping into the living room. She was wearing pretty pink pyjamas covered with teddy bears, and she had long, glossy, black hair which was gleaming as though it had just been washed. She jumped on to the sofa and threw her arms around Patrick's neck, then snuggled her loveable round face into his chest. Patrick was in a state of shock. Still suffering from the effects of all the alcohol he had drunk, he initially thought his sister Sandra had somehow got into the flat with her little daughter Kerry. But this child was nothing like Kerry, by any stretch of the imagination.

"Who are you?" Patrick finally managed to stammer.

The little face looked up into his astonished face, her beautiful large green eyes staring right into his. "I'm your daughter, Daddy," she said, with a serious expression on her face, "but I haven't been born yet."

As Patrick tried to digest the strange reply, the girl vanished before his eyes, yet for a while he could still feel the child's weight on his lap and chest, and smell her fragrant, newly-washed hair. He stood up, suddenly feeling stone-cold sober, and wondered if his friend Steve had spiked his drink with some narcotic substance. He went to bed, and twice during the night, he distinctly felt the phantom child hugging him. He was more fascinated than afraid.

Over the next few nights he had very vivid dreams that he was with the little girl, and in one dream, the child begged, "Daddy, please find my mummy, or I'll never be born!

Please, Daddy!" Then the child started to cry her eyes out. Patrick promised her that he would do as she asked, and he woke with hot tears stinging his eyes. What was happening to him? Was he losing his mind? Who was the sweet little child who kept on calling her Daddy? He decided to tell Steve about his strange experiences, as he was the only friend he could confide in. But, Steve was not the fanciful type – he didn't believe in dreams and the supernatural – and Patrick's attempt to pour his heart out, went straight over his sceptical friend's head. "What you need is a session down the pub," was his unhelpful response.

"No, I'm sick of all that," said Patrick, angrily. "What's the point?"

Steve stopped smiling, "Okay, you're on your own then," he snapped. "You're losing it, mate."

For months Patrick had been saying that he was going to go back to college, but for some reason he hadn't been able to motivate himself to actually go and do it. Somehow, his strange encounter with the little girl had given him the impetus he needed. The following day he got up early and set off for the local further education college, where he enrolled on a computer course. He quickly found that he had an aptitude for computers and was soon doing so well that it was clear he would be able to find a career in IT. Whilst he was there, he was introduced to a pretty young student called Paula, and started dating her. The relationship quickly became serious, Patrick had never met anyone like her before. They married in July 2000.

In May 2001, Patrick, who was now in full-time employment, became the proud father of a little girl whom he and his wife decided to call Amy. She was born with a full head of glossy, black hair. His wife and baby daughter have transformed his life, and he is absolutely sure that the spirit of his unborn daughter somehow crossed over into the aimless, layabout world in which he was living, to help her future father change the direction of his life.

THE LAST TIME I SAW CLANCY

Over the years, many people have asked me if there was any truth in the story about the dog that swam across the River Mersey in the 1950s. I asked the public for information about this incident many times on the radio, and from the accounts received, I have pieced together the following tale.

In the early 1950s, thirteen-year-old Paul was strolling past one of the farms that used to exist off Childwall Valley Road, when he noticed a hand-written sign hanging on the fence saying: 'Labrador Puppies For Sale. Enquire within'. Paul had always longed for a dog of his own, and when he saw Farmer Jackson rolling a milk churn down the lane, he eagerly ran up to him and asked how much he was selling the pups for.

"Six shillings each," said Jackson, gruffly, as he hoisted the heavy churn up on to the stone platform outside the farm gate. As he was shutting the five-bar gate, a sleek black Labrador emerged from the kennel, with six tiny pups tumbling after her. A seventh pup trailed behind and seemed to have trouble walking. It was very skinny and weak-looking and was half the size of the other six. "I've only got two shillings, Mr Jackson," said Paul, pulling out a handful of coppers from the pocket of his shorts and laboriously counting it out.

In a cold voice, the farmer replied: "Well, you'll need another four, son. They're all pure Labradors."

As Paul turned disconsolately away from the gate, the farmer called him back and grudgingly said, "Go on then, give me what you've got, and take this one." Jackson pointed to the seventh pup, the skinny one that was staggering around the yard on its wobbly little legs. Paul was reluctant at first, and asked the farmer why it had such difficulty walking. The farmer scooped up the puppy and handed it to Paul. "She was the last of the litter, the runt, that's why she's so small. Make your mind up. Do you want her or not? I haven't got all day."

As soon as Paul held the tiny furry bundle in his hand he was smitten, and handed over his two shillings. Farmer Jackson tutted at the handful of ha'pennies and pennies, but Paul didn't even notice. He stroked the tiny puppy, which looked at him with its big round eyes and licked his fingers.

On his way home, Paul met Clancy Jones – a girl he had a crush on. She made a huge fuss of the pup and to impress her, Paul said that he would be naming her Clancy. She was very touched and gave Paul a quick peck on the cheek. His heart fluttered as he watched Clancy walk on down the lane.

When the boy returned home with the pup, his widowed mother was furious. She could just about afford to keep herself and Paul, never mind a sickly dog. Paul was crestfallen, but at least she had said that he would be allowed to keep the pup for a few weeks, until she had found someone she could give it to.

A week later, Paul's spinster aunt in Waterloo died unexpectedly, and in her will, she left her house off Crosby Road to Paul's mother, and this house had a garden back and front. Barely able to believe their good fortune, Paul and his mother moved into the house, along with Clancy. The dog soon grew stronger and started to walk properly, and Paul used to take her to the park each day for a long runaround.

Paul and Clancy became inseparable, and Paul soon realised that the animal had more senses than the average dog. She had amazing hearing and also seemed to be able to tell the time, because each evening she would look at the dial of the clock when it was 5.30pm, and would run to the hallway, waiting for Paul's mother to come home.

In 1952, Paul had been fantasising that he was a prospector in a log cabin in Alaska in the hut at the bottom of the garden. He fell asleep reading his comic by candlelight. When the candle burnt down to its base, the hot wax soaked into the wooden tabletop and ignited.

Meanwhile, Paul's mother was in the kitchen, making the tea, when she saw something amazing. The hose-pipe had been left unwound in the back garden, but left attached to the standpipe. Clancy had the end of the hosepipe in her mouth, and had it trained on the hut, which was billowing smoke. Paul's mother rushed out and forced the door open. Paul was dragged out coughing and spluttering. They hugged each other, realising what a close escape he had had.

However, Paul and his mum were baffled as to who had turned on the tap to feed the hose-pipe – surely Clancy wasn't that clever – but they soon discovered that she was. In the summer, they watched her craftily tilt her head and grab the tap with her teeth and turn it on. She would then seize the end of the hosepipe and playfully spray the water about, aiming it especially at the cat next door. Clancy was very crafty and only did this when she thought no one was watching.

On another occasion she went missing, and Paul and his mother found her sitting on a neighbour's doorstep, staring solemnly at the door. The old woman who lived there often gave Clancy fish scraps on a Friday, but this was a Sunday. The dog began to howl at the door. Paul and his mum had never heard Clancy make such a weird, mournful sound. Later that day, the old woman's daughter entered the house and found her mother lying dead in bed. She looked very peaceful and had a slight smile on her face. It turned out that she had died that morning, but how did Clancy know that?

In the summer of 1953, on Paul's birthday, he went to the

Pier Head, ready to embark on a voyage to New Brighton with his cousin and a friend. With him, on a leash, was Clancy, carrying a plastic bucket in her mouth. Long before the ferry arrived, a gang of bullies confronted Paul and one of them snatched a bag of sweets from him. Clancy sensed that the gang's intentions were to harm Paul, and she growled at them. The biggest member of the gang put the sole of his foot on the dog's back and cruelly pushed her through the safety railings. Paul held on to Clancy's leash, but her collar slipped off. The tide was in and the waters of the Mersey were high, and she yelped as she tumbled into the muddy, swirling waters. The strong currents soon carried the dog out into the Mersey, with Paul watching helplessly from the bank.

A group of adults chased off the bullies and tried to comfort Paul. He pushed away from them and watched Clancy's head bobbing up and down in the choppy water. It looked as if the dog was trying to swim against the current towards the opposite shore, in an effort to stop herself from being washed out to sea. Paul and his cousin boarded the ferry to Birkenhead, hoping that Clancy would make it to the other side of the river. When they reached Birkenhead, they checked the waterfront, and a woman told them that a dog had crawled up the stone steps to the promenade about twenty minutes before. She had tried to go to the animal's aid but it seemed very afraid and ran off. Paul and his cousin scoured the area, but could find no trace of Clancy.

Then Paul came upon a terrible sight; staring out of the back of a dog-catcher's van, was the unmistakable face of Clancy, still wet and bedraggled from his heroic swim. He and his cousin dashed after the van but failed to reach it.

Paul's mother didn't have a telephone, and he never thought about going to the police. He and his cousin caught the ferry back to Liverpool, then boarded a tram home, where they told his mother about the bullies and Clancy's ordeal. The next day she visited the local dogs' home and the RSPCA and made enquiries about a black Labrador, but was told that there were no dogs of that description in the kennels. Paul was so distraught, that he and his mother ended up travelling back to Birkenhead to search for Clancy. When they finally located the kennels, the dog catcher sadly shook his head and said, "I'm sorry, love. I'm afraid the Labrador was put to sleep. She was in such a bad state. Been in the river by the looks of things." Paul and his mother returned to Liverpool with heavy hearts, knowing that they would never find another dog like Clancy.

Paul is now in his sixties, and tells how, about a year after Clancy died, he was awakened in the early hours, by something licking his hand. In the dark he could just make out the familiar face of Clancy. It wasn't a dream, or any kind of hallucination; the dog was there – he could feel her and smell her. The face of his devoted canine friend then melted slowly away.

GHOSTLY BYSTANDERS

In 1997, thirty-five-year-old Greg from Bootle left his girlfriend's flat on Sheil Road just after three o'clock in the morning. He put on his safety helmet and mounted his 250cc Honda Super Dream motorcycle and drove off into the freezing cold night. Greg travelled up Belmont Road, turned right into Breck Road, and then, seeing that Priory Road looked deserted, he gave his motorbike full throttle and accelerated as he performed a wheelie, with the front wheel of the bike in the air. As Greg tore past Stanley Park, his bike seemed to hit what felt like a stretch of black ice, and he lost control of the machine, then hit a brick wall. It all happened so fast, it seemed unreal.

Greg woke up surrounded by a crowd of bystanders. He immediately realised that his left arm was paralysed, and assumed that it was broken. Both of his legs felt completely numb. He groaned and one of the bystanders – an old man with a white moustache and a flat cap – leaned over Greg and said, "Hold on there, son. Help will come soon."

Greg looked to his left and saw a woman of about fifty years of age looking down at him. She wore a long black dress that went down to her ankles. She was smiling at Greg, and she suddenly whispered something that annoyed and terrified him at the same time. "He's a goner," she said, to no one in particular. "The shock'll kill him." A few other members of the crowd that Greg couldn't see muttered in agreement with the morbid woman.

Greg reached inside his leather jacket with his uninjured hand and frantically felt for his mobile phone. His hand shook as he retrieved the phone, and he held it out to the old man and said, "Phone for an ambulance. Quick." The old man recoiled from the phone as if it were a gun. He gazed at it with a puzzled look and said nothing in reply. Greg couldn't understand why the old man refused to take the phone from him. He offered it to another man standing over him, but he too just stood there without accepting the mobile. Then something happened which threw a supernatural light on to the proceedings.

There came a sudden gust of wind which disturbed the flowing, ankle-length skirt of the woman who had predicted that Greg wouldn't survive the crash. There were no feet or shoes at the end of that skirt when it fluttered in the wind – just empty space. Only then did Greg realise that the people surrounding him were not people at all, but ghosts. Twenty feet away from where he lay was the wall of Anfield Cemetery. When Greg gazed up once more at the face of the woman, she was gazing down at him with a grinning expression that made his flesh creep.

A hackney cab suddenly screeched to a halt at the scene and the taxi driver jumped out and knelt beside Greg to reassure him that he'd just called for an ambulance. Greg pointed to the figures, which were now slowly dispersing, but the cabby obviously couldn't see the ghostly bystanders. Greg watched as each of the figures left the scene of the crash and walked, one by one, back through the wall of Anfield Cemetery.

Within the space of a few minutes, an ambulance had arrived and, after treating Greg at the scene, they took him away to hospital. He survived the crash, despite his very serious injuries. He told the staff at the hospital about the ghosts who had surrounded him after the motorbike smash. One of the nurses revealed that many years before a similar incident had taken place at the same spot. A motorist who had crashed on Walton Lane was brought into casualty, and he swore that the crowd of bystanders who had come upon the scene before the ambulance had slowly melted away as the paramedics arrived.

THE MAN IN BLACK

One evening in 1932, on the night of a full moon, nine people arrived at a house in St John's Road in Waterloo. Some of the nosier neighbours, twitching their net curtains, wondered what the nature of the gathering was. Was some party imminent perhaps? Was it somebody's birthday? Had they known the truth, they would have been scandalised, for the people were actually assembling for a séance. It is an ancient belief that the number of people attending a séance should be divisible by three, and so these nine people from Waterloo, Crosby and Litherland seated themselves around a large round table in an upstairs room, ready for what some of them regarded as a bit of fun, and others as an adventure into the unknown.

In the centre of the table was a loaf of bread. Bread placed in the middle of the table in such a way is also part of an age-old custom, and is thought to attract the spirits for some obscure reason. Three candles were lit around the bread, and the heavy velvet curtains were drawn and overlapped so that not even a single ray of moonlight could enter the room. The men and women each spread their hands out on the table so that they touched one another by the tips of their little fingers. The participants then intoned these words together: "Spirit, we bring you gifts from life into death. Commune with us, spirit, and move among us."

Everyone present waited eagerly for a response. Two raps from the spirit were expected, and the sitters waited in tense silence. This was the first time a séance had been held at this particular address on St John's Road. Other séances held by the group at other addresses had all been huge anti-climaxes. Little did anyone know that this address held a terrible dark secret; this was a house where supernatural dabblings should definitely not have been carried out.

The sound of a clock striking midnight could be heard in the living room downstairs. The candles started to flicker on the table, and as the midnight chimes started to fade, everyone felt something vibrating through the table. The floor and the entire room began to shake. Then, suddenly, the curtains flew fully open as if pulled apart by invisible hands – to reveal a sinister figure in a long black cape standing there. The strange outdated figure was seen as a silhouette because of the full moon shining down behind it through the window. It flitted forward towards the startled people at the table, and it placed its hand on the shoulder of the man acting as the medium of the table. This man shuddered because, even through his clothes, he could feel that the hand of the supernatural stranger was colder than ice. Everybody then gasped in fear and amazement as the figure vanished instantly with a loud flutter of its cape.

The gas lamps on the wall were quickly lit, and everybody wondered what the significance of the sinister vision was, and why it had touched the medium's shoulder. Everybody agreed that the man in the black cloak had given off a strong aura of evil which had permeated the whole room.

The next morning, the medium from that séance – who lived in Crosby – was found dead in his bed, and on his pallid face, was a look of the utmost horror. The case then deepened when other participants discovered from various people in St John's Road that the house had a reputation for being haunted. The man in black had put in an appearance at least forty years before, and was reputed to be a harbinger of death.

Now, I was intrigued to receive a letter in early 2003 from a Mrs Stephenson who once lived at the haunted house in Waterloo, but who now lives in Australia. She said that, in 1976, a female relative was returning home one night, just after nine o'clock, and as she entered the house, which was in total darkness, she noticed a faint glow at the top of the stairs, and silhouetted against this glow was the figure of a man in a cape. The woman froze in fear, and cried out, "Who's that?" When there was no reply, she realised that she was seeing the spectre she had often heard her mother talk about. It was supposed to appear when one of the family was about to come to harm. On previous occasions it had put in an appearance before the death of her grandmother, and on another occasion it had materialised days before her brother had suffered a heart attack.

The woman panicked because she was convinced that the phantom was going to attack her. It definitely gave out a strong impression of menace. When the woman switched the light on, the figure instantly disappeared. Nine days later, the woman's brother was seriously injured in a car crash, but fortunately recovered. The figure was about 5ft 10in in height, had short black hair, and wore a cloak that covered its legs.

In 1987, Mrs Stephenson emigrated to Australia with her family and young daughter. Then, a few years ago, she returned to Waterloo, and during the visit, she and her brother and daughter went to visit the old house on St John's Road to reminisce, and during the visit her daughter disappeared. She had wandered off by herself into a room upstairs. This girl had never been told about the incidents with the man in black. When her mother caught up with her, she was trembling. Something had obviously upset her. She told her mother that a man's voice had urged her to pick up a piece of glass which was lying on the floor from a broken window, and to use it to slash her wrists. He had then added: "It won't hurt; you will only feel cold for a short while."

Mrs Stevenson had heard enough. She grabbed hold of her daughter's hand and pulled her out of the accursed house.

The identity of the man in black remains a mystery.

CORA VERSUS THE GHOSTS

In December 1975, thirteen-year-old Cora and her forty-five-year-old mother Jackie, moved into a house in the Islington area of Liverpool. Cora's father had died three years previously from a heart condition, and her mother still hadn't really got over her loss, or found anyone who could take his place.

At Christmas, Cora received a lot of gifts from her mother, aunts and grandmother, and among these was the distant ancestor of the Play Station – a primitive electronic video game called 'Pong'. The game was an electronic version of ping-pong played on a domestic television screen. The ball was nothing more than a square blip that bounced back and forth across the television screen between two on-screen paddles that could only move up and down when the players turned two corresponding dials. The ball made a loud bleeping sound when it bounced off the paddles. A child today would quickly tire of such a rudimentary video game, but in 1975, children – and adults – happily played Pong for hours.

One evening Cora and her friend Sally were playing Pong as they chatted about boys, clothes, pop songs, and similar topics that teenaged girls often talk about. Sally's mother called at the house at 9.30pm to say that it was time for her daughter to go home. Sally left, and when Cora went back into the living room, she was surprised to hear the bleeping sounds still coming from the Pong video game console. The paddles on the screen were moving up and down, and the ball was ricocheting between them. Something was playing with the video game.

"Mum!" shouted Cora, and she turned and ran into the kitchen where her mother was doing the washing up. Cora excitedly told her about the strange incident taking place in the living room and urged her to come and have a look for herself. Grabbing a tea towel and wiping the suds from her hands, Jackie followed her daughter into the living room. The white luminous blip of the ball beeped as it bounced randomly across the screen. The paddles were stationary now. The ghost, or whatever it was, had ceased playing with the game.

"Something was playing the game, Mum. I swear!" Cora said, with obvious sincerity.

Jackie had never known her daughter to lie, and felt uneasy as she listened to Cora's spooky account.

Cora and her mother retired to their beds at 11pm, but at three in the morning they were awakened by a low rumbling sound that seemed to shake the whole house to its foundations. Jackie leapt from her bed and ran downstairs, thinking there had been a gas explosion or an earth tremor, but downstairs everything seemed fine. Jackie could find nothing to explain the earth-shaking phenomenon. As Jackie left the living room, she bumped into Cora, who had also crept downstairs to investigate the origin of the tremor. Jackie yelped with fright and Cora giggled and apologised.

Cora went back to bed, and her mother returned to her own bedroom. Cora had only been asleep for a few minutes when she woke up and saw that the walls of her room were moving inwards, closing in on her. She tried to rationalise what she was seeing, knowing that logically it was impossible. Yet the room was definitely getting smaller. Not only that, but the teenager found that her whole body was paralysed, and she began to suffer a sensation of being suffocated. As she struggled to breathe, a putrid, stomach-turning odour assailed her nostrils, making her want to retch. She had the sensation of something pressing down on her, and in her mind caught glimpses of bodies lying about in heaps, some actually lying on top of her. The room grew darker and, suddenly, the voice of a young boy screamed out, "Connie!"

Cora started to pray, fervently muttering the Lord's Prayer, and almost instantly, the bedroom walls reverted to normality, and the unpleasant sensation of pressure on her body vanished, along with the filthy smell. Cora sat bolt upright in bed, gasping for breath, then quickly got up and turned on the light.

Several days later, Cora's friend Sally was sitting in the front parlour of the house, browsing through a magazine, when she suddenly had the eerie feeling that she was being watched. She cautiously looked over the top of the magazine and there were three figures: a boy, aged about ten, a girl of about sixteen, and an old man. They were all dressed in old-fashioned clothes. Their faces looked very pale and sickly, and their eyes were dark and sunken. Sally let out a strangled scream and the figures vanished.

Cora came running into the parlour and instantly noticed the same rank smell that had manifested itself in her bedroom during the terrifying episode that had occurred a few nights before. Sally refused to stay in the parlour and quickly left the house after telling Cora what she had seen. Cora's mother Jackie saw the ghosts of a young boy and a teenaged girl days later, standing on the stairs, mournfully gazing at her with those creepy dark eyes. The figures slowly vanished as Jackie looked on in shock. Jackie suggested to her daughter that perhaps they should leave the property as it was obviously haunted, but Cora was a very brave and determined girl, and she said that she wasn't going to be defeated by a bunch of ghosts; she was going to fight them.

Cora set off for the Central Library and read everything she could find about exorcism. She scooped holy water into a bottle from the font in the local church, and borrowed a large, wall-mounted crucifix and a family Bible from the home of her grandmother, who was a devout Roman Catholic. An ornamental bell which she found in the house would also be of great use in the rite of bell book and candle, which she had read about in the library. Jackie urged her daughter not to dabble with supernatural matters and still thought they should leave the house, but the child was adamant about confronting the ghosts. They were preventing her from sleeping, they had scared her best friend out of the house, and they simply did not belong there.

Jackie put her hands to her face and sat trembling in the living room as Cora performed the exorcism. She splashed holy water about as she quoted from the Bible. Many candles were lit, and Cora held the crucifix out at the places where the ghosts had appeared. Closely following the instructions in the library book, she said aloud: "I abjure thee and summon thee to leave this place in the name of Jesus Christ!"

Weird groaning sounds started to fill the house, and a musky smell circulated on a draught which came from nowhere. Jackie called up the stairs and pleaded with her daughter to stop the exorcism rite. She shouldn't be dabbling with forces she didn't understand. But young Cora took no notice. The bell was rung, which seemed to stir up the sinister breeze and it attacked the candles, making their flames splutter. After the longest hour in Jackie's life, her daughter, looking pale and drawn, finally came downstairs and declared, "It's okay, Mum. They've gone and they won't be back."

She was right. The ghosts never did return. Perhaps it was just imagination or autosuggestion, but on the following day, when the sun shone, the rooms in the house all seemed brighter, and a fresh, sweet aroma unaccountably permeated the air. Sally was eventually persuaded to return to the house, and her friendship with Cora continued to blossom. Today, Sally and Cora are still the best of friends.

What kind of supernatural forces had been haunting the house? Well, an old woman called Maggie told Cora's mother that the house had had a spooky reputation for some time. Maggie's mother had told her that the area of Liverpool where the haunted house stood had once been consumed by a deadly cholera epidemic. In that quarter of the town, the dead were brought out and thrown on to a cart piled high with decaying bodies. Groans were sometimes heard to come from some of the bodies, so the cholera victims obviously weren't always dead when they were taken away to the secret burial pits.

Apparently, a grandfather, his grandaughter and grandson, who had lived at the infamous house, had succumbed to the plague, and their bodies thrown on to a cart, atop the tangled knot of other corpses. Not long afterwards, it was said that the phantoms of the three were seen and heard at the empty house. Over the years, the visitations had become less frequent and intense. So what had provoked the sudden recurrence of the hauntings was not known, and Cora was never able to find out.

However, Cora researched the story which Liz had told her, and discovered that in 1849, Asiatic cholera visited Liverpool. In a crumbling old book, she uncovered this eyewitness account of the epidemic:

People were dying all around me in dozens; neighbours might be talking at their front doors at dusk with each other, and by morning most would be dead. Every morning a cart would come round, preceded by a man with a red flag, who cried, "Bring out your dead". No coffin was there, not even a shroud, as the corpses were lifted out of the cellars and kitchens. Anywhere they fell stricken, and were thrown on to the cart. Two or three might be taken from one house, and on several occasions I heard moans from the bodies as they lay in the cart, showing they were not dead. They were all carried out to Bootle to be interred without shrouds or coffins in a common grave.

Cora researched the cholera plague incident still further, and discovered that in 1849, the year of the outbreak, sixty-nine-year-old George Green had lived at her house, along with his grandaughter Connie, aged fifteen, and her brother Alfred, aged nine. Cora cast her mind back to that night when she had felt the walls closing in on her and the awful sensation of being squashed under a pile of bodies. She had distinctly heard the sound of a boy crying out the name Connie.

Cora and her mother moved from their home in the 1980s, and today the house no longer stands.

Residential Ghost

To earn some money during the summer school holidays, seventeen-year-old Penny from Wirral, took a job at a local residential home for the elderly. Situated at the end of her road, the attractive building had always intrigued her, standing, towering and stately, on the corner of the meandering pathway through to the park. She passed it every day on her way to and from school, and had always wondered what it must have been before it became a residential home.

On the first day she started work as a temporary care assistant, she was extremely nervous, cautiously making her way up the gravel path towards the brass knocker on the intimidating red, double-fronted main door. Her echoing knock seemed to shake the very foundations of the place, and she heard heavy footsteps approaching the door. She was greeted by a stern but friendly matron.

On that first day she noticed that the framed photographs lining the walls in the entrance hall showed that the building had been used as a hospital during and after the First World War, but she couldn't quell her romanticised imaginings of the fabulous building having once been some artistocrat's abode, bustling with society's élite, with the kitchens and ground floor hectic with busy servants.

She settled into the job with no problems, and enjoyed helping the elderly residents. Often, she would even go in and visit them on her lunch break. Many of them were real characters, with interesting stories of the past to share with any young and eager ears willing to listen. Quite a number of them were bed-ridden for one reason or another and glad of the company, if anyone could find the time to pop in with their afternoon cup of tea and join them for a few minutes.

It was during one of these particular visits that Penny first learned the history of the building and its original owners.

It was an old lady called Muriel who had lived in the area since childhood, who remembered the tale which her mother had told her about the wealthy landowner who had lived in the building in the early 1900s. Indeed, it had been a grand house belonging to a widower who lived there with his only daughter, Emily. A lively young girl, with bright blonde ringlets and a prettily dimpled chin, she had the run of the huge premises, including the vast and blooming garden where she particularly loved to dance and play.

Muriel's voice softened as she explained that years later, in the 1950s, the house had been renovated, and where the kitchen extension now stood, there had once been a raised well, where Emily, despite her father's repeated warnings about the dangers of playing near the well, had made many a wish and thrown many a coin in hope and expectation. That well was also where Emily fell one summer afternoon, as her father busily tackled a bundle of mail in his study. Apparently, nobody heard her scream as she stumbled to her doom. The servants chatting in the basement as they loaded the pantry with the recently-delivered fresh meat, the maids in the parlour polishing the silver before dinner, the cook in the kitchen preparing a rich stock for the last meal of the day, were all too busy to hear Emily's fading cries.

Emily's petite body lay slumped and lifeless at the bottom of the deep well for many hours, while her mystified father searched for her late into the night. Muriel explained to Penny in hushed tones that the poor father had been devastated by his second terrible loss. It was said that the ghost of little Emily still haunted the long corridors and hallways of the old house, searching for a friend to play with.

Muriel's tale sent a shiver down Penny's spine. She

glanced at her watch and realised that her shift had started again some minutes ago, so she rushed back to work and the haunting story was pushed to the back of her mind. That was until a few months later when she was working an evening shift. The nursing home was short-staffed and Penny found herself working the shift with just one other girl, Tracy, and the matron in charge. With one less member of staff, they were run off their feet, and Penny only had a chance to call in very quickly on Jane who had been ringing her buzzer every five minutes since she had started that evening. Trying to do several jobs at once, she dashed to Jane's room to see what was the matter.

Jane was paralysed from the waist down and so could not get herself out of bed. As Penny walked into her dimly-lit room, she smiled; Jane looked so cosy all tucked up in bed, ready to go to sleep, but she opened her eyes on Penny's entrance. Penny noticed that her room was cool and so went to shut the window, thinking that she had probably been ringing to complain of the cold, but it was Penny who turned cold when she heard what Jane was about to say.

Jane drowsily explained to her that she was really tired and needed to get some sleep. Penny agreed that it was late and that she must be weary. Jane then continued by saying that although she had enjoyed the nice conversation she had just had with the little girl, she would like her to leave now. Penny was at first confused. "What little girl?" she asked, as she tucked under the bedclothes at the bottom of her bed.

"The pretty one," Jane said, sounding a little frustrated. "The little girl with the blonde ringlets. She's lovely but I am really tired now and she must leave me to sleep."

Penny knew that no visitors had entered the premises that evening, and as it was after nine o'clock, it was unlikely that anybody would call so late. She stiffened as Muriel's story flooded into her memory. Jane was of sound mind, so Penny was deeply unsettled by her claim, but humoured her anyway.

"Well, I'll ask her to leave now and let you sleep, and if she comes back, why don't you try and ignore her to make her leave," Penny suggested, her body still icy at the thought of the ghostly child. She pulled Jane's door tightly shut and tiptoed back along the narrow, creaky corridor to the winding staircase and made her way down to the staffroom, where Tracy and Matron were both sitting.

"You look pale, love!" Tracy exclaimed. "Are you okay?"

Penny stared at her and then started to smile. "Yes," she shrugged, "it was just something weird Jane said, claiming a little girl was in her room or something, maybe she's losing it …" she added quickly, trying to make light of what had just disturbed her, but her voice faded as she noticed the expressions on both women's faces drop.

Matron cleared her throat and sighed, "Poor Jane …" she whispered. "Let's hope it's not true this time."

Penny was startled, "What do you mean?" she asked.

Matron and Tracy exchanged meaningful looks and then proceeded to explain how both of them had also heard a similar story to the one Muriel had told Penny about the little girl in the well, but the sad tale didn't end there. Apparently, it had become a kind of folklore in the home, that little Emily visited residents who were close to death, almost like a guardian angel. Practically all of the residents since Matron had worked there (some fifteen years) had referred to a small blonde girl, usually around the time their health took a turn for the worse.

"Did Jane really say that?" Tracy asked, expressing doubt. "I've heard the rumours, but I didn't believe them."

Penny also didn't want to embrace such a dark notion, so evaded her question and busied herself for the rest of her shift, trying to put the awful idea out of her mind.

It wasn't until she came back to work for the Christmas break that she noticed Jane's room was empty. Matron explained that a few things had changed since she had last been in work, including Jane's condition. She had been taken to hospital the week Penny had last spoken to her, just after she had told her about the blonde girl. Her health had deteriorated dramatically and she had never been well enough to come back to the home.

Worse still, as Penny stood in the kitchen area wiping away a tear, and Matron leaned over to pass her a tissue, she noticed a huge round crack in the floor tiles, directly underneath the large wooden table. Another deathly chill flashed down her spine as she wondered if that could be the outline of where the dangerous old well had once stood.

PHOTOGRAPHIC POLTERGEIST

According to the Occultists, there is more to photographs than we realise. They not only contain the image of a person, but they also contain some essence of the subject's soul. Shamans and witch doctors from many of the so-called primitive tribes of the world refuse to have their photograph taken because they believe that the camera is able to steal a part of the soul. It's easy to laugh at these superstitious beliefs, but there may be a grain of truth in the claim. Witches in the West and practitioners of Voodoo, use effigies of an enemy and snippets of their adversary's hair to harm them. Sometimes, just having the name of a foe was enough to harm him or her through the use of magic. A painting of a person was also occasionally used by the practitioner of the Dark Arts to cause injury or death by supernatural means.

When the exact image of a person became available through the science of photography – a science that Occultists say was once known to the ancients but subsequently lost – better results were achieved by the malevolent spell-casters. This idea of photographs having supernatural properties would throw some light on the following strange cases.

In 1994, a woman named Irene told me that she had experienced poltergeist phenomena at her home, centred on an old cupboard in her kitchen. The middle drawer of the cupboard flew across the kitchen into the hallway one afternoon, and the startling incident was witnessed by almost a dozen people who had just attended the funeral of Irene's grandmother. I inspected the contents of the drawer and found they included an old photograph album containing snaps of Irene's late grandmother, and several children. In the same drawer there was a reel of cotton thread, a small piece of purple card that held a collection of sewing needles, and a frayed cloth tape measure.

When I opened the photograph album, a colour photograph of an elderly man dropped out. Irene explained that this was a recent snapshot of her grandfather, William, who was now living in a retirement home. She had decided to put his photograph in the album – which she had only recently found in her late grandmother's bedroom. It had seemed fitting to put William's photograph in the old album, because, curiously, there were pictures of his late wife and her three younger sisters in the book, but there were no old pictures of William on any of the pages. Irene's grandmother had separated from him twenty years before, so Irene assumed that was why her grandfather had not been included in the family album.

I had a strange hunch about this. I examined the photographs of the three children, whose ages ranged roughly from about nine to twelve, and noticed that two of them were upside-down. Irene was quite shocked when this was pointed out. The photographs were mounted on the page by means of four, forty-five-degree slits, which held the corners of the snaps, so surely someone must have deliberately turned those photographs upside-down? No, they hadn't, as we soon learned.

The photographs were righted by Irene, and the snapshot of her grandfather was put back in what she considered to be its rightful place in the album. The album was then put back in the drawer, but on the following evening the cupboard shook violently and Irene watched as the drawer vibrated and gradually eased itself out of the cupboard until it clattered on to the floor. When she picked up the photo album, she discovered something quite shocking. Two of the sewing needles that had been attached to the piece of card, had now impaled the photograph of her grandfather William – through each of his eyes! What's more, the photographs of the three children were now missing from their page. Instead, they were on the front page of the album, loosely sandwiched together.

Irene visited her grandfather at the retirement home and told him about the strange goings on regarding the photograph album. The colour immediately drained from his face and he gasped for breath when he heard about the eerie episode. A couple of tears trickled from his eyes – he was visibly upset.

A week later, William's health suddenly deteriorated, and his condition quickly became so serious that a priest was called in to administer the Last Rites. Before his death, William asked to see Irene and, in a weak faltering voice, admitted to her that he had once been a cruel bully to his wife's three sisters, who had been much younger than him. He had been twenty-five at the time and they had been aged eleven, twelve and fourteen. Through a set of tragic circumstances, the sisters had been forced to move in with Williams's seventeen-year-old wife – their eldest sister.

Further investigation revealed that William had raped the eldest of the three sisters after a drunken brawl and had almost blinded the youngest when he struck her viciously with the buckle of his leather belt in an unprovoked attack. The sharp buckle had almost ripped off the girl's eyelid. One of the girls died from meningitis, and the other two perished in a blaze that was allegedly caused by a carelessly-discarded cigarette at William's house. It was widely rumoured that William had deliberately caused the fire.

After listening to this deathbed confession and researching into her family background, Irene was drawn to the weird conclusion that the poltergeist phenomenon might have started because some kind of essence contained in the photographs of the three sisters did not want to share the album with the snapshot of the hated brute who had made their lives hell.

PHOTO OPPORTUNITY

Another uncanny story involving a photograph took place back in the early 1980s.

In February 1981, twenty-seven-year-old Jayne Walker from West Derby, received a Valentine card from an admirer who later confronted her in the Philharmonic pub as she was enjoying a drink with friends. Her admirer was thirty-five-year-old Ronnie Saunders who was a bricklayer, and lived just a few streets away from Jayne. Ronnie had fallen for the petite red-head from the moment he had set eyes on her, and Jayne had had her eyes on the tall and stocky raven-haired Ronnie long before he had even noticed her.

The couple got on very well, and in May 1981, Ronnie took Jayne on a holiday to Paris, not just for the romance of it, but because Liverpool Football Club were due to play in the city against Real Madrid at the Parc des Princes stadium. Although she was an ardent Evertonian, Jayne attended the game with Ronnie. The final score was Liverpool 1, Real Madrid 0. A late goal by Alan Kennedy ensured that the trophy would remain in England for a fifth year. As the ecstatic Kop left the scene of the victory to the strains of *You'll Never Walk Alone*, Jayne and Ronnie went for a quick drink then headed back to their apartment at a hotel on the Rue de Saint Petersbourg.

In the hotel lounge, Ronnie got into a heated argument with a Spanish guest named Jorge Zorone, who had also just been to the match. He unwisely claimed that the Hungarian referee had shown favouritism towards Liverpool and that this had swayed the result. A diplomatic French guest at the hotel intervened and calmed down the Liverpudlian and the Spaniard, and Ronnie and Jorge ended up shaking hands and discussing sport in the hotel bar.

Although Jayne loved her boyfriend, she secretly thought that Jorge was the most handsome, athletic-looking man she had ever seen, and when she was introduced to the Spaniard, she felt a shiver of delight when he bowed, took hold of her hand and kissed her knuckles. His dark eyes had a twinkle of mischief and passion, and his smile had an innocent genuineness about it, which she found irresistible. He gallantly declared that Jayne was a perfect example of a beautiful English rose, and told a story about his grandfather, Vincent Zorone, a man who had won back the hand of his red-haired sweetheart after killing her lover in a fencing duel.

"Her hair was as red as yours, like a flame," Jorge said, grabbing a lock of Jayne's long hair and squeezing it in his fist as he grimaced, as if in pain.

At this, Ronnie decided that they had seen quite enough of Jorge for one night, and firmly took hold of his girlfriend's hand and told the Spaniard that he and Jayne were now going up to their room to get some much-needed sleep. Jorge seemed genuinely sad to see Jayne leave, and watched wistfully as Ronnie pulled her along after him as he went to the elevator. Jayne turned back, gazed dreamily at Jorge and gave him a feeble wave. The elevator doors parted and the English couple entered the lift, which took them to their room on the fifth floor. As it happened, Jorge Zorone's apartment was on the same floor, just four doors away down the corridor.

At four o'clock that morning, Jayne woke up after hearing a strange clicking sound and seeing a bright light momentarily flash through her closed eyelids. She awoke, and immediately the strong scent of Jorge's after-shave drifted under her nose. A voice next to her, somewhere in the darkness whispered, "Jayne, I love you. Come away with me."

Jayne recoiled with fright as Jorge's face suddenly loomed closely over her. She wondered about the click and the flash, and groggily asked, "Did you take a photo of me just now?"

"No, my darling. You must have dreamt it."

"Look, I don't know what you want, but if you don't get out of here this minute, I'll wake up Ronnie, and he'll knock you out," whispered Jayne between gritted teeth.

Jorge backed off and silently left the apartment. Jayne was left wondering how Jorge had managed to gain access to the hotel room, and was creeped out by the whole episode, despite her earlier opinion of the handsome Spaniard.

The next morning, Jayne decided that it would be wise to say nothing about Jorge's intrusion into the bedroom, it would only cause an almighty row, and someone might end up getting hurt. However, much to Jayne's relief, the lecherous Spaniard seemed to be making himself scarce at breakfast. At around 10am, Ronnie and Jayne were finishing packing their suitcases, when Ronnie cried out in agony and collapsed on the bed. He writhed around and told Jayne that he felt very hot and was finding it difficult to breathe. The hotel manager was summoned, and he in turn called for a doctor. The doctor examined Ronnie, and confirmed that he was running an abnormally high temperature. He was obviously suffering from some kind of fever, but the doctor couldn't be sure what it was. He needed further tests, but since they were going home that night, the doctor advised seeking medical help when they got back home. The strange thing was that the fever suddenly ceased after half an hour and Ronnie recovered with no ill effects.

Shortly after all this, Ronnie and Jayne were down in the foyer arranging for a taxi to take them to the airport later in the day, when the hotel manager began a lively discussion in French with the assistant manager. Jayne knew a little French, and gathered that the assistant manager was saying that a guest had stolen a number of room keys. The police soon turned up and after talking to the manager, they took the elevator to the fifth floor. Ronnie and Jayne went up to their own room about ten minutes later. As they passed Jorge's room, they noticed that the door was open, and they could hear the raised voices of the two policemen, quizzing him over the keys he had in his possession. Jayne hung about in the corridor, staring in at Jorge and the police officers, determined to find out what was going on, but Ronnie urged her to stop being so nosey.

Jayne was about to walk on, when she noticed something which chilled her to the bone. On a table in the room, just by the door, was a candle which was slightly burned down, and in front of it there was a polaroid photograph of Ronnie – asleep in bed. Jayne immediately thought back to the nocturnal visitation by the creepy Spaniard. She had been convinced that she had heard a click followed by a flash of light which had penetrated her eyelids. It must have been been Jorge taking a picture. She was so outraged that she walked right into Jorge's apartment and tried her best to tell the policemen about the photograph and how the Spaniard had somehow gained access to her room without their permission. Jorge cursed her in his native tongue, and his handsome face seemed to be transformed with evil. The police inspected the photograph of Ronnie and noticed that it was singed in the centre by a candle flame. The photograph and candle stood upon a piece of paper upon which strange symbols had been scrawled all over it.

When Ronnie was shown the partly scorched snapshot, his blood ran cold, and he angrily asked Jorge, "What's your game, eh?" But the police intervened before Jorge could reply.

The Spaniard was arrested for stealing several spare keys to rooms in the hotel and was soon led outside to a waiting police car and taken off to the station. The hotel manager had no idea what Jorge had been doing with the photograph, but Jayne was sure that he had been carrying out some sort of black magic ritual, using Ronnie's photograph to harm him. The way Ronnie had burned up with the mysterious transient fever led her to believe that it was Jorge who had inflicted the condition, through supernatural means. The Liverpool couple booked out of the hotel that evening and were only too glad to return home.

Be careful who you give your photographs to …

Sentimental Journey

Billy Marston had a very special knack for remembering things in great detail, because his work demanded it. A considerable part of his job as a painter and decorator was to work out estimates, and to then recall what materials would be required, and in what quantities and measurements, without the need to even note them down. Billy remembers the date of the following strange incident in every detail, even though he was eighty-nine when he related his account of it to me.

It was Monday, 11 November 1974. Every newspaper, every radio and television news programme was full of the mysterious disappearance of the Earl of Lucan. The vanishing lord had abandoned the car he had used to flee from London at Newhaven on the south coast. Detectives had hoped to catch up with the Earl to determine whether he could help them with their inquiries into the 'Upstairs-Downstairs' murder of the Lucan children's nanny, and the attack on Lady Lucan. The elusive Lord Lucan has still not been found to this day. Much was made of his vanishing act in the media at the time, and he became quite a household name.

As one mystery unfolded in London on that rainy November night, another one was about to commence two hundred miles further north in the Mossley Hill area of Liverpool. At around 9pm, at the Rose of Mossley, sixty-year-old bachelor Billy Marston, was lost in thought as he leaned at the bar, his cloth-capped head bowed over a half-empty glass of Mackeson stout. Billy was thinking about the past and, at the same time, worrying about the future. A painter and decorator by trade, he was increasingly finding that much younger men were being employed in the painting and decorating business and he was finding it hard to compete.

Anyway, it wouldn't be long before he was drawing his old age pension. Where had all those years gone? and what had happened to all his friends and relatives?

Once upon a time, many years ago, he used to go out on dates with attractive women, and had lots of friends and brothers and sisters. But, sadly, he was now the sole survivor of his family and most of his friends had gone away to other areas, lost touch with him, or died. His best friend Mulhearne had died suddenly a year ago from heart failure. It had been a terrible shock and made him feel old. Julia, the sister who had been closest to Billy since childhood, had died from cancer five years before that. With a deep sigh, Billy downed the last dregs of his glass of stout, and said goodnight to the barman. He left the pub and wearily trudged down Rose Lane towards his home, the way he did most nights, back to his lonely and rather neglected house on Woodlands Road.

As Billy trudged along through the soft drizzle, he was engulfed by melancholy as he contemplated the bleakness of his life. He was giving in to self-pity, when a man came walking out of a side street and startled him. In a low, professional-sounding singing voice the stranger sang a song which Billy hadn't heard for years. The song was *Sentimental Journey* and dated back to the 1940s. The first verse floated through the damp night air:

> *Gonna take a sentimental journey,*
> *Gonna set my heart at ease,*
> *Gonna make a sentimental journey*
> *To renew old memories.*

The stranger's youthful stride quickly put increasing distance between himself and Billy Marston, and in less than a minute, he was a fleeting figure, barely visible through the drizzle as he flitted up the lane, but he could still be heard whistling the wistful melody as he melted into the shadows of a large oak tree's overhanging branches.

Billy slowed down, the words still ringing in his ears. He knew the song well and it had struck a chord in him. "That sounds like a good idea," he muttered to himself, "I think I'll take a sentimental journey of my own."

His mood immediately lifted. He turned, and walked off in the opposite direction with a renewed sense of purpose. He had decided to revisit his old neighbourhood on Penny Lane. He was filled with the need to go on a sort of pilgrimage, to pay some homage to the golden years of his life. There are mental states of heightened alertness in the human mind of which we are hardly aware. The alpha, beta, delta rhythms of the mind as it sleeps, pays attention, or meditates, are fairly well known to neurologists, but this state of heightened consciousness was completely alien to Billy. It was almost euphoric, yet mystical.

As he reached the corner of Briardale Road and Penny Lane, he turned right, and as he did so, he found himself back in the world of 1929. The drizzle had gone and Billy felt fifteen again. Stiff joints, rheumatic twinges and eyes blurred by cataracts were no more, he felt sprightly, energised and fully alive. And bliss! The teeth in his mouth were his own again. The cloth cap had inexplicably vanished from his bald pate, to reveal a mop of thick blonde hair.

He immediately noticed that the shops on the lane were the ones that had been there in the 1920s. They had all shut up for the night, but he noted all the old, familiar painted signs above their fronts. Then Mrs Bruce, one of his aunt's neighbours, came down the lane. As she shuffled past him, she said, "You'd best be getting home, Billy. You young gallivanter." Billy gazed at her in awe, but felt impelled to walk on, for he instinctively knew that if he was to allow himself to doubt that he was back in the late 1920s, for even a second, the spell would be broken and he would be back on the rainy night-time street of 1974.

He walked on as if in a dream. The distinctive low moaning sound of a rolling tramcar brought a smile of recognition to Billy's face. It sailed into view, rocking gently from side to side up Smithdown Road: a tram with a ghostly, gas-lit interior. Shadowy figures were both seated and standing in its saloon, heading for the terminus. Cobbled roads stretched before him where tarmac had lain in the dreary decade he'd left behind.

He crossed the road, hopping over tram lines worn shiny by a non-stop stream of trams ferrying their passengers to and from the city centre, and made his way to the home of his youth on Charles Berrington Road. He unbuttoned his overcoat and removed his scarf; it was a lovely warm evening and felt like summer. Downwind, on a gentle breeze, came the delightful, memory-jogging aroma of Ogden's mellow pipe tobacco. Two old men, Mr Godley and the meerschaum pipe-smoking Mr Greene, stood on their neighbouring doorsteps chatting, or 'chinwagging', as they used to call it back in the twenties. They were discussing Lancashire's recent win by ten wickets against South Africa at the three-day match at Liverpool Cricket Club, in Aigburth. Billy noted everything they said as he passed by.

Further up the road he passed old Mrs Brown's front parlour window and heard her playing a truly haunting melody on her old upright piano. It was Hoagy Carmichael's *Stardust*. In 1929 Billy had courted a beautiful girl named Violet who had loved that song. Filled with nostalgia, the music tugged at his heartstrings and he felt the full force of the emotions he had experienced at the time. He resolved to call at her home in a short while, just to hold her in his arms one more time.

Billy gazed up at the jewelled, velvety sky and whispered a few very apt lines which he had remembered from the song Mrs Brown was gently playing:

High up in the sky the little stars climb,
Always reminding me that we're apart,
You wandered down the lane and far away,
Leaving me a song that will not die.

A red-nosed drunk with a rakishly tilted bowler hat embraced clung to a lamp-post as he howled out *Old Man River* – shattering Billy's reveries.

Billy paused as he approached the bay window of the front parlour he knew so well from long ago; the front parlour of his own old house, where he had lived until his marriage at the age of twenty-two. An overwhelming emptiness suddenly came over him, damping down the euphoria that had so far accompanied his sojourn into the past. His poor, working-class mother and father and sisters lived at the house, and they had barely been able to scrape together a living in those lean times. Billy wished he could somehow convert all of his savings in 1974 into the currency of 1929 and stuff it through the letterbox.

He stood in the shadows, gazing at the house, afraid to knock on the familiar door. He knew that if he entered that house, he would never be able to leave again. It would simply be too emotional to pay a flying visit, and something deep down told him that this stroll into the past was due to end at any moment.

Then, suddenly, the front door opened. Billy's heart thumped wildly inside his chest, as his mother leant down and put the empty milk bottles out. The family's old, one-eyed cat, Nelson, brushed past her and sauntered out into the street. The cat arched its back when it caught sight of Billy's silhouette lurking outside the lamppost fringe of illumination. "Mum ..." the faint word barely escaped from Billy's choked-up throat and drifted into the night air unheard by his beloved mother.

The door closed and Billy heard the sound of a bolt being drawn inside. He looked down at his old cat and bent down to reach out to him saying, "Nelson. Here, puss. Do you know who I am?" The cat hissed and ran off into the night.

Billy silently said goodbye to the house and walked away with scalding tears cascading down his cheeks. He stopped on Heathfield Road, his emotions once again in turmoil. He stared at the window of Violet's bedroom. He knew that his first love was sleeping there, unaware of everything. The thought of tossing a handful of gravel at the window crossed his mind, but he knew that he had no right to confuse her – he must let her be.

A policeman was approaching on his beat along Smithdown Road. It was time to leave. "I will always love you, Violet," Billy whispered, eyeing the drawn curtains behind which his eternal sweetheart lay sleeping. He could almost hear her singing the words of *Stardust* in his mind. Violet would die from a brain tumour in three years time ...

Billy sorrowfully retraced his steps back up Penny Lane, until he reached the corner where his amazing journey into the past had begun. He knew that he couldn't stay, and silently accepted the fact without protest. He was too upset to object. Whenever he had reminisced publicly about the good old days, people had told him he'd been looking at the past through rose-tinted spectacles, but now he knew that he hadn't. Now he knew exactly what he had lost – those carefree, halcyon days when his greatest worry had been what to wear on his dates with his sweetheart, Violet.

As he walked up Briardale Road, the stiffness of old age gradually returned to his joints and his vision clouded over once more, as the cataracts covered his eyes. A modern car sped past, then another – gone were the virtually car-free streets of the 1920s. He had returned to 1974 and the noise and bustle of the busy streets around Penny Lane confused him.

When he arrived home he sat in silence for a while, ruminating over the night's events. He could not be sure that he wasn't going mad. How on earth, and for what reason, had he been allowed to go back over forty years to the 1920s? It was a question to which he never found an answer.

The next day, out of the blue, Billy was visited by a cousin with whom he'd lost touch. Andy had travelled from St Helens specifically to find Billy, and admitted that his motivation for seeking him out had been loneliness, because he no longer had any immediate family. He had then remembered his cousin who was about the same age as himself. Perhaps because they were both in the same situation, Billy and Andy got on famously and chatted into the small hours about incidents from their early lives. Here was a real-life link with the past. They still had a great deal in common; so much so, in fact, that Billy soon invited Andy to live with him, and they made a pact to build a proper social life for themselves.

They began by paying a visit to the local crown green bowling club. Not only did they both enjoy the game and find that they were good at it, but they also met two women who took them off to ballroom dancing classes. Lonely nights and self-imposed isolation became a thing of the past for the two cousins and suddenly their old age did not seem so bleak after all. As an added bonus, all the exercise seemed to help Billy's rheumatism, and his painful, creaking joints eased.

Shortly after relating his touching timeslip tale to me, Billy Marston passed away, aged eighty-nine. He struck me as a very honest and straightforward man, and he earnestly assured me that the trip into the past really did take place, but he was at a loss to explain why or how it happened. What is apparent is that that night appeared to be a turning point in Billy's life, and from that time onward, he seemed to find his way again.

A SOLDIER'S RETURN

One stormy winter's night in January 1919, thirty-year-old Rose Griffith was sitting in the front parlour of her house in the vicinity of Newsham Park, playing an old seventy-eight record of *Roses of Picardy* on her horned Decca gramophone. Rose was passionately singing along to the crackling record. She knew all the words off by heart:

> *Roses are shining in Picardy,*
> *In the hush of the silvery dew,*
> *Roses are flowering in Picardy,*
> *But there's never a rose like you!*

Rose's cousin Margaret turned up at the house that night. She was concerned about her cousin's increasingly eccentric behaviour, which had started when Rose had learned that her husband Ivor had been killed during the Battle of the Somme, three years before. That battle, which started on 1 July 1916 and ended on 13 November of that year, had been the bloodiest episode of the First World War, involving

1,353,000 troops representing thirty-five nationalities. The great River Somme winds its way from the centre of Picardy to the Channel coasts, and even today, the name of the area remains a byword for futile and indiscriminate slaughter.

Margaret had heard about Rose's strange behaviour from neighbours in her street in Kensington. They had told her how Rose always left her back yard gate and back-kitchen door open, as she expected her late husband to come home any day. Before the war, he had always come through those doors when he returned home from work, and Rose claimed that, even after death, her deceased husband had returned several times to see her, and he had entered the house via the back yard and back-kitchen doors.

Rose looked a sorry state. Dark circles ringed her sad, sunken eyes, and when she sat talking about her beloved dead husband, she would wring her hands and rock slightly backwards and forwards. It was obvious that her thoughts were focused solely on her husband and she would repeatedly glance at the parlour door with an expression of expectation, as if she thought that Ivor was about to enter at any moment.

Margaret tried to talk some sense into Rose. She brewed a pot of tea and whilst she was in the back-kitchen, she attempted to close the door, as it was freezing cold and the open door was chilling the whole house. But, without saying a word, Rose immediately walked into the kitchen and opened it again. "Look, Rose, Ivor will not be coming home tonight, tomorrow, or ever again," Margaret said, gently taking her cousin's hand.

Rose was still looking past her and towards the back-kitchen door. She answered her cousin very calmly. "No, you're wrong, Margaret," and as Margaret silently embraced her, Rose quietly added: "He still comes to see me."

Margaret shook her head, she could see that she would

have a very difficult job convincing Rose that the best thing would be to try and forget the awful loss of her husband and try to get on with her life. The two women sat in the parlour drinking tea for the remainder of that evening, and the storm outside showed no signs of abating. Rain and wind swept into the back-kitchen and Margaret drew nearer to the living room fire in an attempt to keep warm, whilst Rose remained oblivious to the rising chill and disruption in the room. Thunder rolled and lightning flashed through the scarlet parlour blinds.

At 11pm, suddenly Rose started humming a tune. She rocked back and forth in her chair, gazing vacantly into the dying embers of the coal fire. She then began to sing. "Roses are shining in Picardy, in the hush of the silvery dew," her eyes were bright and sparkling as she sang to the dwindling flames.

Margaret sighed and bit her lip. It was almost unbearable to watch Rose suffering so badly and she decided that it was time that she left, as there was nothing she could do to alleviate her misery; her cousin seemed beyond help. She was just putting on her coat and hat when there was a distant thump from the rear of the house. It sounded like the back yard door being slammed shut – probably by the gales. Then there came another slamming sound. This time there was no mistaking it – the back-kitchen door had just been closed. Rose immediately stopped singing and jumped to her feet. "Darling!" she exclaimed, a wide grin spreading across her face.

Margaret watched her cousin's reaction to the noises and was alarmed. She felt distinctly uncomfortable as her concern for her cousin increased. The sound of heavy footsteps coming up the passage outside made Margaret jump to her feet too. The tread of boots came right up to the parlour door, and the knob of that door squeaked as it slowly turned. The two women stood transfixed, scarcely daring to breathe.

The door opened, and by the pale luminescence of the glowing gas mantle, they beheld the figure of a soldier, dressed in a mud-spattered British Army uniform, and looking weary and dejected, as if he had just emerged from the trenches. The figure stepped forward across the threshold of the parlour, and as he did so, Margaret let out a scream of absolute terror, because she could now clearly see that the soldier's face was gruesomely disfigured. Parts of his face were missing. There was a jagged, yawning black socket where his left eye should have been, and a section of exposed jaw and missing teeth on the lower side of his face, completed the horrendous picture.

Rose did not seem to be aware of the soldier's horrific injuries and stepped forward to embrace the terrifying apparition of what she obviously recognised as her husband. Margaret threw her hands up in fear and covered her face as she dashed past the ghostly soldier. She ran through the hallway and left through the back door. She ran out into the bleak back alley in the lashing rain without daring to even look behind her.

From that evening onwards and for the rest of her life, Margaret refused to go back to the house near Newsham Park.

LADY ON THE LEDGE

There is a block of inner-city apartments in Liverpool that was completely renovated in the late 1990s, changing it from one of those hard-to-let properties, into one of the most desirable addresses in the city. When the luxury dwellings became available, they were soon snapped up by young, upwardly mobile people keen to get on the property ladder and secure a trendy apartment for themselves in the city. However, neither the landlord, nor the unsuspecting new residents, knew about the eerie ghost that haunts the building.

The first realisation that something supernatural was at large occurred one night in 1999, when a professional couple, Greg and Susannah, were watching television in the lounge with all the lights switched off. The time was 9.45pm, and the only lights that illuminated the apartment, apart from the flickering television screen, came up from the sodium street lamps in the road below, filtered through the vertical blinds.

"What was that just then?" asked Greg, jumping up from the sofa. He stood stock still, gazing at the window.

"What was what?" Susannah asked, staring at the same window in the hope of finding some kind of clue as to what he was going on about.

"Someone just walked past that window outside. It was a woman. She must be on the ledge," Greg gasped, and he cautiously parted the silver vertical blinds and peered through.

"You what?" Susannah said, unable to hide the doubt in her voice, as the apartment was five storeys up. "How could there be anyone out there. The ledge is too narrow. They'd be killed."

A narrow ledge, which was, in fact, just about big enough to walk on, did run around the building, but why would anyone risk their life walking along it at night?

"There's someone out there! Look!" said Greg, getting increasingly exasperated by his partner's attitude.

He tried to open the window to give the suicidal ledge stroller a piece of his mind, but Susannah always kept the double-glazed windows locked. As Greg went to fetch the key, Susannah also saw a young woman in black walking past the window. Her face was extremely pallid, almost blue, and her eyes looked dark and sad. On her head she wore a ladies' 1930s-style hat with a velvet pleated drape and bow. She also wore a black jacket and a calf-length shirt – not the sort of clothes to go climbing the outside of buildings in. She was bare-footed, and she walked slowly and deliberately along the narrow ledge without even acknowledging Susannah's presence.

As soon as Susannah set eyes on the lady in black she felt there was something ethereal and other-earthly about her. Greg returned with the key and quickly unlocked the handle on the window. He swung open the window and gazed along the ledge just in time to see the woman jump off the ledge. Greg recoiled from the window in shock, the vision he had just seen indelibly printed in his mind. He expected to hear a sickening crunch as her body smashed into the pavement below, but he heard no such sound.

As the colour drained from his face, he told Susannah what he had just witnessed, and she became very agitated. She suspected that the woman was actually a ghost, and her hunch proved to be right.

As Greg ran downstairs to check if the woman had fallen to the pavement, the same figure walked past the window once more and this time looked in at Susannah, who screamed and ran out of the flat. She was so terrified that she ran down the five flights of stairs in her bare feet. On reaching the pavement outside she flung herself into Greg's arms, and the two of them stood there looking totally bemused. The woman in black was neither there, nor up on the ledge.

The ghost was later seen by several other people in the same block of apartments, and the same terrible scenario was played out before their eyes. Then, for some reason, the ghostly female made herself scarce for several months. To this day, no one is certain who exactly the ghost walking the ledge and repeatedly jumping off it could be.

A woman named Theresa, who lives on the fourth floor of the apartment block said that on one occasion she actually saw a woman's body plunge past her window. Perhaps the suicidal shade is the ghost of someone who took her own life from that ledge in the 1930s, but, up to press, I can find no record of such a suicide from that period.

Because of strained nerves after the experience, Susannah and Greg left their apartment and moved into less trendy, but much more congenial accommodation in Woolton village. The ghostly lady apparently still walks precariously on the ledge and then jumps to her 'death', and was seen as recently as March 2002.

A CABBIE'S TALE

It was Autumn 2002 and just another November night on the taxi rank for Mike, a cab driver with over twenty years' experience of the hackneys. His cab was parked in the rank on Bolton Street, which runs from Copperas Hill and the north side of the Adelphi Hotel, to Skelhorne Street and Lime Street Station. Business was slow, and Mike chanced going to fetch himself a cup of hot black coffee from the café that caters for cabbies, situated just thirty feet away. Then Mike returned to his well-kept vehicle, and climbed into the driver's seat. He was just about to remove the safety lid from the polystyrene coffee cup, when he noticed a tall, gaunt-looking man in a long dark coat approaching from the direction of Lime Street Station.

Mike's cab was second in the queue of hackneys lined up in Bolton Street, and as the man crossed Skelhorne Street in his approach to the rank, the cab in front of Mike moved off. Mike gave up on his coffee and placed the cup in a holder on the dashboard. The man in the long black coat seemed to glide up to the vehicle in a most unnatural way, and what's more, he seemed to be muttering to himself. At closer quarters, the man looked about fifty-something, yet fleet-footed and agile. As he entered the cab, he said to himself, "I didn't quite get that."

"What was that, mate?" Mike asked, assuming the fare was talking to him.

The man impatiently waved his hand, dismissing Mike's query as a trivial distraction.

"That's all I need," Mike thought, an eighteen-carat nutcase talking to himself. "Where to, mate?"

The man looked up and closed his eyes for a moment, then in a deep, rich sounding voice he said, "Clubmoor. Yes, that's it, driver. Take us to Clubmoor!"

Mike wondered who the 'us' the well-spoken man was referring to could be. "Clubmoor? Er, what part of Clubmoor, sir?" he queried.

"I'll tell you soon, bear with me."

Mike began to doubt whether it was worth setting off and took him to task. "What d'you mean, 'bear with you'? What's the address?" and he swung round in his seat and glared at him.

His creepy passenger scowled back at him. "Look, driver, I don't expect you to understand what I am about to tell you …"

"Don't call me driver; it's Mike; and why wouldn't I understand? Go on, try me," said Mike, his patience thinning.

"Very well …" the man leaned forward, ready to explain. "I have just come by train from Manchester. I am a medium, and I was in the middle of a séance when it was interrupted by a spirit with some urgent information. The information was vague and incomplete, but my spirit guide is helping out now."

Mike gave him a blank look and muttered, "Oh, I see."

The man continued, "My name's Justin, and I swear every word I tell you is true. My guide, Augustus, is sitting next to me now, and all this is a matter of life and death."

Mike detected an air of sincerity in the man's voice which made him believe that he was not some crackpot after all. He had been feeling bored on the quiet taxi rank, so he decided to give this adventure a whirl. "Okay, Justin. I'll drive to Clubmoor and you can tell me what what's-his-name tells you."

"It's Augustus," said the psychic, urgently. "He's a bit faint tonight. He says Clubmoor and he is showing me a name with the word 'ash' in it. It's a street in Clubmoor. It could be Ashmont or Munash – sorry it's a bit vague."

"Monash Road is in Clubmoor …" Mike said, gazing in his rear-view mirror as he turned up Skelhorne Street.

"That's it – Monash, and I even have the number on the door," Justin said with a smile. "Driver … I mean Mike … a woman's life may depend on this. It's a rather long-winded story, but in short, the woman is an old flame of mine, and the spirit of a relative of hers broke in on the séance to say that her life was in danger. A man with a knife is watching her."

Mike cursed the red traffic light under his breath, then sighed as he realised that he hadn't reset the meter. "Man with a knife?"

The medium seemed deep in prayer with his hands clasped together and his eyes closed tightly. He didn't say anything for almost five minutes. Mike pushed his vehicle to the limits and made Monash Road in record time. "Here we are, mate."

Justin sprang from the cab and scanned the numbers of the doors until he came to the numeral which had been relayed into his mind by Augustus. He called at that address, and waited. He could hear someone moving behind the door, and he could see the tiny point of hallway light – just visible through the wide-angle door-viewer – blink off.

"Mary it's me – Justin! Open the door!" said the medium.

He heard the sounds of a chain being unfastened, and of a bolt being drawn back.

The door opened, and there was Mary, a woman Justin had not set eyes on for over a decade. When she broke off their romance, the sensitive medium had almost been destroyed by the heartbreak. Tonight she stood there gazing at him in surprise with a slight smile as she recognised him.

"Justin!" she gasped, stepping back into the hallway and invited him in.

Justin turned to the cab driver and called, "I won't be a moment."

Mike nodded, and waited. He sipped his now lukewarm coffee and shook his head, grinning at the extremity of the unusual tale he had been told so far.

Then there came an insistent tapping on the cab window. Mike turned, startled, to see a man of about thirty standing there. His head was shaven and his eyes had an intense, unsettling stare.

"Who was that man who just went in to Mary's place?" he demanded.

"I don't know, mate. Why?" Mike replied.

"I'm her husband … that's why, mate," said the man, who was obviously very agitated. Suddenly he produced a hunting knife, then turned to stare at the front door of Mary's home. "She's always bringing men back and it's got to stop," he said, to himself rather than to Mike.

As soon as the man moved away from the cab, Mike lost no time in calling the police on his mobile, as he felt a dangerous domestic incident was about to unfold. Within ten minutes the police were at the scene, and the knifeman, who was pacing up and down outside Mary's house, fled when he saw them arrive, but he was soon caught on Queens Drive.

It turned out that Justin's supernatural tip-off had been correct. For over two months, Mary had been stalked by a man who had convinced himself that he was married to her. The stalker had a history of being obsessed with women, but had only ever been cautioned. Mary was amazed at the way Justin had turned up at her address through information imparted by a spirit. It had been the spirit of her uncle, who had always watched over her in life, and who was now apparently doing so in death as well.

Justin paid Mike for the unusual trip to Clubmoor, and told him that he would be staying with Mary overnight to calm her nerves. He would try his utmost to persuade his former love to move with him to Didsbury on the outskirts of Manchester.

A week later, coincidentally – or perhaps there were mysterious forces of synchronicity at work again – Mike and his wife went to the Puschka restaurant on Rodney Street to mark their tenth wedding anniversary. Moments after their arrival, Justin and Mary entered and were escorted to a table near the window. Justin spotted Mike and his wife, and he came over to say hello to them. He then returned to his table. As Mike and his wife were getting ready to leave the restaurant later that night, Justin came over and told the hackney driver that he would soon be hearing the patter of tiny feet. "No way," said Mike, and explained that he and his wife had been trying for children for many years without success. However, three months later, Mike's wife discovered that she was pregnant and the couple were overjoyed.

THE DOOR

In this age of emails and the internet, I regularly receive many tales from Liverpudlians who have settled in other countries. This tale from the United States was related to me by Susannah Rye, who left Liverpool with her husband in 1974, to live in Belwood, Illinois.

In 1976, Susannah was getting ready for bed one moonlit summer night. She carried the family cat Sydney down from her daughter's bedroom and was about to put it out, when she saw something which gave her palpitations. Through the glass pane in the front door she saw a man and a woman outside on the porch. He was very tall and broad with a shock of white hair and she was petite and delicate and was wearing horn-rimmed glasses. The man had his large chubby hands around the woman's throat, and he was shaking her like a rag doll as he throttled the life out of her. The fur on the cat's back stood up on end and it darted back upstairs like a streak of lightning. Mrs Rye quickly followed in the cat's footsteps, running up the stairs two at a time to her husband, and gasped out the story of He telephoned the police and then, in typical American fashion, removed his ·38 revolver from his gun cabinet, ready to protect his family.

When the police arrived, they found no trace of the white-haired strangler, or his alleged victim, and for some strange reason, they seemed very subdued and uneasy as they listened to Mrs Rye's description of the people she'd seen on the porch. One of the policemen patted her on the shoulder, and after a long silent pause, said: "Those people you saw, Mrs Rye; they weren't real."

Mr Rye was angry that the police were not taking his wife seriously and demanded an explanation. The policeman awkwardly fidgeted with his hat and replied, "Well, sir. About three years ago, before you folks moved into this house, the people living here saw the same thing – a tall, well-built man with white hair, strangling a very small woman on the front porch. There was also a real murder here in 1966, when a local mechanic strangled his wife. He was a big burly man with white hair and she looked like the lady your wife described ... real small, like a little bird. The murder happened five miles down the road from here."

"If that's the case, then why should we see their ghosts here? Why have they singled out this house?" asked Mr Rye, reluctant to swallow such an outlandish tale.

The policeman said that the front door of the Rye's house had once been the front door of the mechanic's house. The landlord had salvaged it when the strangler's house was burnt down by a lynch mob. The door, which was very attractive – being very old and elaborately carved – was later used to replace the door of the house now lived in by the Rye family.

The policeman's account made the Ryes' skin crawl. Mr Rye lost no time in taking the jinxed front door off its hinges and replaced it with a new one. He offered the old door to his neighbour, Dave Reichart, who had no belief in anything of a supernatural nature.

Dave left the door in his back garden, intending to use it as his front door but never quite got round to hanging it. Three years later, he reported seeing ghostly figures in its glass panes. Dave, his wife, and his US Marine brother, Mike, briefly saw the eerie figures of a man strangling a woman.

In 1983, the ghostly scene was re-enacted yet again in the glass panes of the door, but the new residents of the house, who were born-again Christians, smashed the door up and shattered its panes.

Backpackers' Nightmare

Another tale from America was reported to me by a former Liverpool John Moores University student called John, who now lives in Los Angeles.

In 2002, before he emigrated to America, John travelled across the United States with his friend Rob. In the autumn of that year, John and Rob were camping deep within the pine forests that lie huddled around the pristine foothills of the Ouachita Mountains in South-western Arkansas. A full moon hung overhead, and the two young men sat around their camp fire, chatting about the day's events. Twinkling in the distance were the lights of the small college town of Arkadelphia, which has a population of about ten thousand, and is the epitome of small town America. In the opposite direction the cliffs lining the Ouachita River were clearly visible, with the moon reflected in the quietly flowing waters far below.

Upon this autumnal night, shooting stars rained from the sky, and while John and Rob looked up in wonder at the heavens to take in the celestial fireworks, they both heard the faint sound of someone sobbing, somewhere in the distance. The crying did not come from the direction of the town – it came from somewhere deep in the forest. About a minute later, the two young men heard a faint rustling sound approaching. A figure darted past them. By the flickering light of the camp fire, they saw that it was a woman dressed in a long black dress. Covering her face was a black veil, and as she moved along she bowed her head as she sobbed.

The young men followed her from quite a distance, as they suspected that there was something sinister about the sobbing night stroller. The woman in black walked for some ten minutes, and John and Rob followed her to the edge of a cliff overlooking the river. They soon realised what the eerie woman's intention was. She looked up at the moon – then jumped! John and Rob watched in horror as her body hit the rocks below – and then seemed to evaporate into thin air. Not even the faintest splash was heard. The men looked at one another in horror and disbelief, then rushed back to their car and drove over seventy miles to another spot where they could rest for the night, but they got little sleep, because neither could stop thinking about the ghostly woman they'd seen.

On the following day they talked to people in the area about the suicidal shade, and were told that the place where they had seen the ghost was haunted by an apparition known as the Lady in Black. It was said to be the restless ghost of a young woman named Jane, who had been a student at Arkadelphia's Ouachita Baptist University in the 1920s. The students of Ouachita University had always competed with the students of Arkadelphia's other acclaimed university – Henderson. It was unheard of for any students from these two universities to mingle socially, and in the 1920s, Jane, from Ouachita University, began to date a young man named Joshua, a student of Henderson State University.

Unfortunately, Joshua's friends held the same prejudices as the rest of the population, and soon began to ostracise him and threatened to never speak to him again if he didn't end his romance with Jane. Joshua eventually succumbed to the pressure, and broke up with Jane on the night of the annual homecoming dance at Henderson. The girl was inconsolable. Her friends tried to tell her that it was for the best, but she pushed past them all and ran away in floods of tears. Her friends became very concerned about her emotional state.

Jane ran up to her dorm room, where she put on a black dress and a veil which she had recently worn at a relative's funeral – then headed for the steep cliffs over the Ouachita River, where she could put an end to the intense, unbearable heartbreak of the break-up with Joshua. She had decided that she could not live without him.

Not long after her suicide, Jane's ghost was seen hurrying to the place of her death by many people in the area, including Joshua. The ghost of the Lady in Black has also been seen haunting the campus of Henderson State University – looking for her lost love. They say her ghost still walks to this day.

When John and Rob heard the story of the Lady in Black, they understandably shuddered. The figure had seemed so lifelike, so real, as carnate ghosts often do.

HOT GOSSIP

In the village of West Derby, in the late nineteenth century, there were four women who had remained good friends since their childhood days. They were Emily Titherington; a red-haired greengrocer, Miss Jessie Moore; a tall and elegant young lady who worked as a draper, the beautiful, angelic-faced Henrietta Colquitt; dressmaker, and Miss Alice Crosby, amusingly described by her three peers as a wealthy loafer. Miss Crosby had never worked since leaving school at the age of fourteen, and had no need to seek employment at all, as she had inherited quite a fortune from her uncle at the age of twelve. However, her mother owned a newsagents and Alice occasionally helped her behind the counter, more for her own amusement than anything else.

All four women were highly regarded as pillars of the

community, but behind closed doors, above Emily's shop on Wednesday evenings, the quartet of young ladies let down their hair to smoke, drink and play poker – in between catching up on the rumours and gossip traversing West Derby's grapevine. During the girls' talk one Wednesday evening, the greengrocer Emily Titherington mentioned a minor mystery that was lapped up and discussed by her friends.

Apparently, a stranger had started coming into her shop on a fairly regular basis to purchase lemons. He sometimes bought apples and oranges, but each week, for three weeks, he had purchased six lemons at Emily's shop. Alice asked her friend to describe this man. Emily said he had light-brown hair, was very tall, aged about forty, and had a comical turned-up moustache. He spoke with a strange accent which she couldn't place.

"That's Mr Glossop," declared Alice, puffing on a cigarette. "He comes into mama's shop for the *Daily Telegraph* each morning. He's very handsome."

Jessie Moore sipped her Gordon's Gin and rolled her eyes knowingly as she noted the look of infatuation blossoming on Alice's face. She delicately licked her lip and asked Alice what else she knew about the newcomer to the village. Alice shrugged and said that no one knew where Mr Glossop was from. Her mother was curious about his background too. Emily Titherington said she felt that he held some dark secret.

"Call it intuition perhaps," the greengrocer said, "but I have uncanny feelings about Mr Glossop."

Without looking up from her poker hand, Henrietta Colquitt said: "Do you mean to say, Emily, that you have never politely asked Mr Glossop about his accent?"

"No I have not," Emily replied.

"How do you know the man's surname?" Henrietta asked.

"He reserves his copy of the *Telegraph* and that's the name mama writes on his newspaper," Alice told her, and she added that Mr Glossop preferred to pick up his newspaper personally rather than have it delivered to his address.

"I wonder what he does with all those lemons?" Emily mused.

On the following day, a smart-looking, tweed-suited Mr Glossop came into the newsagents to pick up his copy of the *Daily Telegraph*, and Alice Crosby was present. She handed over the newspaper and quietly mentioned that she could not place his accent. Mr Glossop said that it was Cornish; he hailed from St Ives. He smiled, nodded politely and left the newsagents. As soon as he was outside the shop, Glossop began to search intently through the pages of the newspaper. He always did that, whereas most customers carried their newspapers home to be read in private.

By the following Wednesday, when the four young women met again in the room over Emily's shop, Henrietta had managed to discover two things about the Cornishman from her brother-in-law, the local postman who had delivered a letter to Mr Glossop. His first name was Augustus, and he lived at Runnymede Cottage, an old dwelling near Sandfield Park that had lain empty for years before he took up residence. Alice revealed that he was from St Ives in Cornwall and added that she had noticed a peculiar habit of his. She explained about the frantic scanning of the newspaper as soon as he bought it, as though looking for something of great personal importance. Emily's contribution to the gossip was that Mr Glossop had been to her shop to buy apples and grapes, but had only purchased a single lemon. She had also noticed that his once light brown hair now verged on being blond.

"That's it! Of course!" exclaimed Jessie Moore, pointing

a finger at Emily. "My mother used to do that. Lemon juice can lighten hair – it's a natural dye."

Henrietta touched the tip of her chin with her index finger and began to meditate on all of the strange facts concerning Augustus Glossop. "Mm, lemon juice. I do believe that our Mr Glossop is trying to alter his appearance for some reason. I think he's got something to hide."

"Do you think he may be a murderer on the run?" Alice asked, with a worried look.

"It's quite possible," Jessie replied, encouraging the suspicion. "Maybe that's why he scans the newspaper so eagerly. He's checking to see if the police are on to him?"

"Perhaps *we* should go to the police ourselves," Alice suggested.

"There isn't one iota of evidence to prove anything," said Henrietta, pouring cold water on Alice's idea. "But perhaps we should check the newspapers though, to see if there is anything relating to a Mr Glossop, or a recent murder committed in Cornwall."

Accordingly, each day Henrietta Colquitt bought the *Daily Telegraph* and scrutinised every page and article, looking for any news of a Cornish murderer on the run. After almost a week of searching, she came across a very curious article concerning the mysterious disappearance of forty-two-year-old Lanyon Tregelly, from Boscastle in Cornwall. Two months previously, in July, Mr Tregelly had gone swimming off the Cornish coast, and had not been seen since. His clothes had been found on the beach, and the authorities had initially presumed that he had drowned, after being swept out to sea by a strong current. However, several people who had known Tregelly had recently reported seeing him at a Bristol train station.

Mrs Tregelly and her three children were heartbroken. If

Tregelly had indeed drowned, it was a tragedy for his wife and family, and if the man had faked his own death, then it was no less heartbreaking for them. Police were keeping an open mind, as Lanyon Tregelly had owed a considerable amount of money to several banks. Furthermore, Tregelly was also suspected of being involved with a Devil-worshipping cult that was thought to have been responsible for a ritual killing of a vagrant. Henrietta trembled when she read that part. The article ended with a short description of Tregelly, and it seemed to fit Mr Glossop exactly – except for his lemon-dyed hair.

Henrietta lost no time in paying a visit to local policeman, PC Kinrade, and she told him about her suspicions regarding Mr Glossop. Kinrade and the sergeant of the local police station called upon Glossop at Runnymede Cottage, and the Cornishman strenuously denied that he was Tregelly and threatened to sue the policemen for slander. However, when a chief inspector visited the cottage with a search warrant, he found two letters from Tregelly's mistress in Cheshire, plus several documents with Lanyon Tregelly's signature upon them. Tregelly was taken back to Cornwall and put on trial for fraud. Lanyon Tregelly was sentenced to nine years hard labour at Dartmoor Prison. No evidence could be found to link him with the occult murder of the tramp though.

Not long after Tregelly's trial, a letter, written in animal blood, arrived at Henrietta Colquitt's home. It was allegedly from a member of the Devil-worshipping cult with which Tregelly had been involved, and the author of the letter promised that he would cut out Henrietta's heart because she had led the police to 'Brother' Tregelly. The Police branded the letter as a hoax, but not long afterwards, Henrietta Colquitt was awakened one night by a strange fluttering sound in her bedroom. She lit a bedside lamp to find a beheaded magpie flying crazily about. It bumped into the walls and furniture, smearing them with blood, and the headless bird even flew into Henrietta's screaming face. How it had got into the room was never established, as all the windows were firmly closed.

This was followed by a succession of uncanny occurrences that ultimately drove Henrietta out of West Derby village.

THE ORMESHER GHOSTS

In May of 1956, a baffling but brutal double murder took place at Number 8 Asmall Lane in Ormskirk, where two elderly spinster sisters, Mary and Margaret Ormesher, lived. Mary Ormesher owned a sweets and tobacco shop in Ormskirk's Church Street. She was a sweet and inoffensive old lady, without an enemy in the world. She and her sister were always helping people out; lending them money, giving the children a few extra free sweets and so on.

On Sunday 6 May 1956, at ten in the morning, Mrs Josephine Whitehouse, a woman who lived in a flat at the back of the Ormesher's shop in Church Street, called at the shop with a cup of tea, as she did every morning, and was surprised to discover that it was still locked up. She therefore set off for the Ormesher sisters' house, a quarter of a mile away in Asmall Street.

Mrs Whitehouse called at the house but could get no answer, so went next door to Number 6, where Mr Thomas Cummins lived. Mr Cummins and Mrs Whitehouse went into the alleyway and through the unlocked door of the back yard. One glance told them that something was amiss; the yard was littered with broken glass from an empty milk bottle and other debris, and the dustbin had also been overturned. Flecks of bright red blood spattered the whitewashed surfaces of the yard's brick walls.

Stepping their way carefully through the broken glass, Mr Cummins and Mrs Whitehouse then gazed through the kitchen window – and there they saw the bodies of Mary and Margaret Ormesher, lying on the kitchen floor, each in her own pool of blood. Mr Cummins pushed against the kitchen door and it opened. After studying the bodies from closer quarters for a moment or two to make sure that they were indeed dead, he ran off to fetch the police; the station was only a hundred yards away at the end of the lane.

Close to the sisters' bodies the police found a leather attaché case which contained about fifty pounds in silver coins. Mrs Whitehouse confirmed that this was the case in which Mary Ormesher carried home the takings every Saturday night. She told how she had always escorted Mary Ormesher to her home with the hundreds of pounds' or so of takings, but last night, which had been Saturday, she had been unable to accompany her, as she had been visiting friends in Southport. There were no notes left in the attaché case and the bundles of paper money that had been secretly stashed in an old grandfather clock had also been stolen. This discovery hinted that it was an inside job. Neighbours said that they had heard noises in the yard that night; a milk bottle being knocked over and a woman's voice crying, "Oh! Mr Cummins!"

A Mr Draper and a Mr Allison both claimed that they had heard the voices on the night of the crime. The two men were neighbours living on either side of the Ormeshers' house. The police investigated the baffling double murder but, despite all the clues, came to a dead end. Every person in Ormskirk over the age of sixteen was fingerprinted – a staggering twenty-four thousand inhabitants. However, frustratingly, no matches were found with those taken from the scene of the crime. Even men who had been on leave from the forces at the time of the murders were fingerprinted at their military locations around the country. Men in the neighbouring towns of Lathom, Burscough and Westhead were also fingerprinted, but still no matches were found.

The case is still unsolved to this day, but it is said that the ghosts of the murdered ladies have been seen on the anniversary of the heinous crime. One who saw the spectres was Frank, from Halewood, who often visits Ormskirk to see his sister. He was brought up in the neighbourhood where the sisters were murdered, and remembers them both clearly. Frank was walking up Ormskirk's Church Street one night, in May 1992, when on the other side of the road, he saw the sisters' ghosts standing near the spot where their old shop had once stood. He was not afraid and crossed over in amazement, but as he approached the figures, who both looked mournful, they vanished before his eyes.

Many people have reported seeing the murder victims' ghosts, and perhaps the shades of the old women will continue to be seen in Ormskirk until their murders are finally solved.

DANCING DEVILS

Many years ago, I was browsing through a second-hand bookshop in Wales when I came across a book that contained the handwritten reminiscences of a Dr Wolfe, who had once had a medical practice in Victorian Liverpool. The conversations which take place between a doctor and a patient in his surgery should remain as confidential as those between a priest and a parishioner in a confessional. However, Dr Wolfe wrote a tract about a bizarre and eerie case concerning one of his patients, decades after his death. Why he wrote the tract has never been determined, but it was certainly never intended for publication.

In the summer of 1884, Richard Maddox, a sixty-five-year-old businessman of Kent Square, in south Liverpool, started to experience alarming hallucinations. These troubling phantasms of his mind first materialised one evening in March, 1884, as Mr Maddox was smoking an after-dinner pipe in his drawing room. The maid had got a roaring fire going in the room and had just brought in some fresh logs. As she was about to leave, Maddox called her back and asked if she too could hear the sound of children's laughter. The maid stood still and listened intently for a few moments, but could hear nothing and soon took leave of her master.

Several minutes after the maid had left the room, a terrifying incident took place. Maddox had gone over to the window to see if there were any children playing in the street, although the laughter seemed to come from inside the room itself. Suddenly, a lurid green radiance flooded the room and turned everything in it a sickly shade of green. He spun round, and was confronted by five small, luminous, green devils, each about two feet in height, dancing and cavorting around the room. The peculiar visitants danced in formation with synchronised movements, and they all gabbled away simultaneously in a strange, unintelligible language, interspersed with high-pitched, childlike laughter. Maddox was naturally appalled by what he saw, and flung his pipe at the sinister apparitions, then ran out of the drawing room in terror.

The maid and another servant listened politely to their employer's account of the green devils and the peculiar green light, but their faces betrayed the fact that they doubted the truth of what he was telling them. In fact, it was obvious to Maddox that they thought he had lost his sanity. Nevertheless, to humour him, they agreed to follow him into the drawing room to see for themselves. When they entered the room they found nothing supernatural at all, only their master's smoking pipe where it had landed on the carpet.

This was not to be a one off incident and Maddox ended up being plagued by the weird, mischievous, glowing imps to such an extent that he was advised by a relative to consult Dr Wolfe, who had been a friend of the family for many years.

Wolfe's initial response, after listening to the far-fetched tale, was to suspect Maddox of abusing alcohol, or hallucinogenic drugs. He said that he knew of a 'blue devils' phenomenon experienced by alcoholics suffering from delirium tremens – the 'DTs' – but Maddox truthfully insisted that he only enjoyed the occasional glass of port. Wolfe then probed further, asking his patient if he took opiates or any other kind of drug, upon which Maddox assured him that he smoked nothing more potent than tobacco. For good measure, when questioned about his lifestyle, he was able to insist that he had not been under any unusual stress of any kind, and that he regularly enjoyed eight hours of sound sleep.

Having ruled out substance abuse and any type of anxiety disorder, Wolfe then wondered if Maddox's mind was succumbing to the early onset of senile dementia, yet his patient seemingly had his full mental faculties intact, and was renowned throughout the city as being a very astute businessman.

Therefore, finding himself at a loss as to a diagnosis, Dr Wolfe suggested a fortnight of complete rest in the countryside, and Maddox readily took the advice, if only to be away from the source of his troubles for a while. The two weeks were blissful; not once was Maddox persecuted by the visions of the horned green gremlins. Even when he was back home it was the same. Before setting off for the country, Maddox had taken the opportunity of arranging to have his drawing room redecorated. The work was not quite finished by the time he returned and for a few days he had to take his after-dinner pipe in the back parlour. After one of these smoking sessions he wrote to Dr Wolfe, thanking him for his good advice, which had apparently worked wonders.

However, a few days later, the work on the drawing room was finally completed and Maddox surveyed the finished room with satisfaction. After puffing on his customary pipe, he had settled down to read a book, in his favourite armchair by the drawing room fire. He felt so relaxed in these comfortable surroundings and breathed a long sigh of relief. His recent ordeal seemed to be over and his peaceful routine had once again been restored.

Then, suddenly, the dreaded dancing devils reappeared out of nowhere and encircled him. They once again danced around him menacingly, gibbering in their strange diabolical tongue, giggling and laughing; obviously deriving some hideous kind of pleasure from the poor man's torment. Maddox felt his heart beat wildly in his chest as he let out a strangled cry and gripped the arms of the chair in terror. The commotion brought all the servants running to see what had happened, but, once again, they could see nothing unusual in the room – only their master, rigid, white-faced and terrified, clinging to the arms of his chair.

The accursed green visitors continued to plague Maddox whenever he entered the accursed drawing room, putting a severe strain on his nerves. His once ruddy complexion took on a pale, waxy hue and his eyes darted about anxiously. His once sturdy frame seemed to shrink and he was soon reduced to a mere shadow of the man he had once been and he would jump nervously at the slightest noise. His decline continued and within a year he died from a stroke.

After the funeral, Maddox's relatives gathered at his house to lament his untimely death. One of them noticed that the curlicued brass fender around the fireplace was new and that it depicted, on its front piece, a head with a face like Pan, the old god of mischief. When questioned, no one in the house was able to say where the strange fender had come from, but one of the maids said that when the coals were lit inside that fender, strange green sparks were often seen.

Was that uncanny fender somehow connected with the tormenting devils that haunted Richard Maddox?

STALKING SKELETONS

Another case of supernatural persecution also has a Liverpool connection. The notes of a Dr R Williams, published in a psychiatric journal in the 1920s, include the history of a wealthy thirty-three-year-old Liverpudlian, only identified as Mr Runcy. In 1899, Runcy was living in the Knightsbridge area of London, and having inherited a large fortune, he was in the fortunate position of not having to work to support himself.

One morning, in July 1899, he awoke with a fearful hangover after a night of hard-drinking with his companions. As Runcy sat up in bed, rubbing his head and squinting at the light filtering through the curtains, he noticed a strange black cat sitting on the carpet facing him. Its piercing eyes seemed to be of an almost luminous cobalt blue, and it sat staring intently at the man of leisure. Runcy was baffled, as he did not own a cat – he didn't particularly like animals – and so he surmised that one of his madcap friends had put the creature in the house as some kind of prank.

However, Runcy soon came to realise that the cat was no ordinary animal, as he was the only one who could see it; the maids, butlers, servants and cooks could not see any black cat, with or without glowing blue eyes, and neither could Runcy's friends.

Wherever Runcy went, the cat did too. He strolled through Hyde Park to try and rid himself of his hangover, and so did the hallucinatory cat. He visited a friend's home in Belgravia, and there was the cat, curled up on the rug, not taking his eyes off his quarry for a moment. Runcy tried to tell himself that the cat did not exist, that it was all some strange figment of his imagination, possibly brought about by the heavy drinking sessions in which he had been indulging, but all the same, the dreaded slinky black phantasm stalked him incessantly, until he was convinced that he was going insane.

Runcy confided in a close friend about the irksome vision, and this friend referred Runcy to Dr Williams, whose West End practice specialised in psychiatric illnesses. Dr Williams ordered Runcy to cease his life of debauchery at once. The all-night parties, the absinthe sprees, the outsized cigars, the rich exotic food and the womanising were to be replaced by a month of total rest and abstinence. Runcy was told to eat simple, bland food and to be in bed by no later than ten o'clock each night.

So worried was the young libertine, that he followed the doctor's orders to the letter and, in doing so, incurred the ridicule of his hellfire friends. However, within a week, the black cat had vanished and Runcy was so relieved that he went to thank Dr Williams in person, after which he returned to his Knightsbridge home with a new spring in his step.

However, his new-found peace of mind was to be short-lived, because as he was walking up the long hallway towards the stairs – a strange-looking man in eighteenth century clothing greeted him. The man wore a small white wig with a ribbon bow tied to its pigtail, and a long crimson satin coat embroidered with an intricate floral design. His black velvet trousers went down as far as the knees, and below that he wore white stockings and a pair of shiny, square-buckled shoes. This outlandish figure beckoned the dumbstruck Runcy with a small sword, which he waved towards the stairs.

"Who the devil are you?" Runcy asked the stranger, but the stranger said nothing, and only smiled in reply.

Runcy soon discovered that the bizarre character – like the black cat – could not be perceived by anyone else, and like the cat, this apparition followed him about everywhere. When he retired to bed at night, Runcy would peep over his blankets and catch sight of the old-fashioned phantom standing to attention in the form of a silhouette against the curtains. In the morning, the figure would still be standing in the same position, waiting for Runcy to rise, ready to resume shadowing him wherever he should go. Dr Williams was most concerned by the new 'ideoform' as he called it, and he arranged for Runcy to be hypnotised, but even hypnosis could not cancel out the imaginary tormenter. Little did Runcy or Williams know that the hallucinatory nuisance would soon be replaced by a truly terrifying apparition.

One Sunday evening, Runcy was walking quickly along Portland Place in the rain, desperately trying to shake off the eighteenth century apparition who accompanied him everywhere. Glancing back, Runcy noted with relief that the street was deserted. There was no sign of the man from his imagination. He rushed homeward, constantly looking over his shoulder and checking the road ahead, but the annoying follower was nowhere to be seen.

Runcy then enjoyed an entire three days free of the man in the white wig and was just beginning to regain his composure, when, on the fourth day, his freedom was shattered. He had ventured out to a theatre in Covent Garden, and sitting next to him was a beautiful woman named Lydia Ellen, a young lady who had many admirers. Runcy was paying little attention to the play, being otherwise occupied whispering sweet nothings into the lovely Lydia's ear, when something suddenly caught his eye. Standing in the central aisle of the theatre, close to the end seat of Runcy's row, stood a tall human skeleton. Runcy stared in horror at the latest apparition borne of his troubled mind. Lydia immediately noticed the look of horror on his face, and followed the line of his gaze to the central aisle – and saw nothing amiss. The skeleton's head slowly turned and faced Runcy; its black eye sockets seemed to penetrate his own and its teeth and jaw formed the frozen grin typical of a skull.

Runcy was so distracted by the skeleton that Lydia soon became irritated, and was convinced that her beau was eyeing some other lady in the auditorium. She was used to being the sole centre of attention and in the end, with a rustle of silk petticoats, she stormed out of the theatre in a huff. The skeletal creature of Runcy's psyche had completely ruined the evening.

Runcy jumped into a hansom cab outside the theatre – and so did the skeleton; its bones rattling horribly whenever it made the slightest movement. He dashed into his home ahead of the skeleton, and slammed the front door. He then breathlessly ordered a puzzled servant to bolt all the doors and windows in the house, but when Runcy reached the drawing room, he saw, to his horror, that the skeleton was already there, standing in front of the blazing fire with its fleshless bony hands clasped behind its curving spine.

Wherever Runcy went, the rattling skeleton followed, and even when Dr Williams suggested a trip abroad, the grotesque figure took the advice too. It stuck like glue to Runcy during his stay in Switzerland, stalking him up the highest mountains and across the deepest lakes.

There is no happy ending to this tale. After almost a decade of persecution, Runcy ended up in a lunatic asylum, and it is said that he died in bedlam. Even upon his deathbed, he saw the grinning face of the skeleton peering between the faces of his family as they attended him in his final hours.

THE MOUTH OF HELL

In a certain part of Liverpool, live two women, both in their early fifties, named Agnes and Joan, who have been the best of friends ever since they were children. In 1999, Joan met a man named Ray, and they got on like a house on fire. Agnes was very pleased for Joan, because she hadn't had a male companion in years – in fact, since her separation from her violent husband. It had shattered her life and left her with deep emotional scars and a complete distrust of all men. Ray started coming round to Joan's on most days and the relationship flourished.

Phyllis was an elderly spinster who lived in the same street as Agnes and Joan. She had the unenviable reputation of being an interfering old busybody. The two friends used to smile whenever they saw her net curtains twitching. Nothing went on in that street that Phyllis didn't know about and she took a keen interest in Joan's new boyfriend.

One afternoon in 1999, Agnes was on her way to visit Joan, when she noticed two men sitting in a car outside her house. As soon as Joan came to the door, they drove off, which worried Agnes, as they had been looking at the house in a suspicious way. The two women thought they might be burglars, casing up the house, and Joan promised to be more vigilant than usual.

By now, she had started a part-time job as a barmaid in a local club, yet was still signing on. A week after starting the job, two benefit fraud officers visited the club and issued her with an ultimatum; either she could continue to work and face prosecution, or she could declare her earnings and continue signing on. She had no choice but to declare the forty-five pounds which she had been paid so far.

A few months later, she had another visit from the DSS, this time at her home. They had been informed that she was co-habiting with a man. Joan tried to look surprised and asked them what they meant. Apparently, a series of benefit fraud officers had been watching her house, and had seen Ray enter each evening and leave at around nine o'clock each morning. Their records showed that these comings and goings had been going on for seven days a week throughout the period of surveillance. Joan had to admit that Ray had moved in. Someone had obviously tipped them off.

The news spread throughout the neighbourhood, and old Phyllis started to avoid Joan. In the end, Joan collared her in the supermarket and accused her of grassing her up. Agnes had to pull her away, as she turned the air blue with swear words.

A few days later, Joan and Agnes were visited by a television licence officer. Neither of the women had a current licence, but Agnes was only cautioned because her television set wasn't in working order, but Joan had to go to court and was fined. That same week, someone put old Phyllis's windows in. There were no witnesses, but most of the neighbours were convinced that it was Joan's act of revenge.

Not long afterwards, Agnes was peeling potatoes in the

kitchen, when she clutched her stomach, doubled up in agony. She had been ignoring a hernia that had been troubling her for months and her bowel was now constricted. She was rushed to hospital, and Joan promised to look after the house while she lay in the surgical ward, waiting to be operated upon. Shortly afterwards, while Joan was minding Agnes's house, she was joined by her nephew Danny. After chatting for a while, Danny became bored and turned on Agnes's computer. Joan told him to leave the computer alone, but then Danny showed her something very interesting. On the screen – written on her word processor – were copies of letters she'd written – and emails she'd sent. There were several emails to the DSS, informing them that Joan was working as a barmaid while still claiming benefit – and one about Joan cohabiting with a man. One email was to the TV Licensing Authority's website – informing them that Joan had no television licence. Agnes had even told the licence people to visit her own house – knowing that her own television was broken and beyond repair. One letter, which had been written sixteen months ago, told a certain electricity company that Joan's electricity meter had been tampered with.

Joan was devastated. She felt as if Agnes, supposedly her best friend, had knifed her in the back. During the course of Agnes's hernia operation, she had a vivid out-of-body experience. She floated out from her body which was lying inert on the operating table, right up to the ceiling, from where she was able to look down, and watch the surgeon and his staff at work on her abdomen. She flinched when she saw the incision and the vivid red blood and watched, fascinated as they were manipulating her intestines. She suddenly felt queasy and floated out into the corridor. At the end of the long hospital corridor, she came across five or six figures, and at first they all looked hazy and out of focus.

Sounding concerned for Agnes's spirit, the figures shouted, "Agnes! Come here! Hurry up!"

Agnes drifted towards them – and could now make out three long-haired men and two women. They grabbed hold of her and started running down another long corridor, which became increasingly dark and cold, and as it did so, the faces of the people underwent a very unpleasant metamorphosis. Their features slipped and slid in a crazy way until they became grotesque, almost like gargoyles. Their fingers changed into claws, which they flexed in and out, as they started to snarl and laugh, revealing long pointed fangs. Agnes cringed as the monstrous devils shouted profanities and revolting phrases that she'd never heard before, and the entities warned her that she was entering the mouth of Hell. One of the women started to sink her fangs into Agnes's back. Then the others did the same. Agnes screamed with the pain as she experienced the sickening sensation of her flesh being bitten and torn away. She closed her eyes and started to pray, and the demons that had hold of her started to laugh, and cried, "Shut up! There is no god."

Agnes started to cry, and pleaded, "Save me, Jesus" over and over, and the demons started to scream at her.

All of a sudden, she felt a comforting, warm sensation, and a light shone at her from the depths of the darkness. In that light she saw the radiant face of an unknown bearded figure and then she saw a second face, and it was one she recognised from the days of her childhood. It was Mrs Blundell, her old Sunday School teacher. On seeing her, the demons suddenly scattered like startled rats into the impenetrable darkness.

When Agnes woke up she was back in her hospital bed on the ward. Sitting by her bedside was Joan. Agnes grabbed her hand and told her of the strange out-of-body experience. Then she confessed to all the bad things she had done in her life –

things that shocked Joan – things that stretched back over years, including all the betrayals which Danny had uncovered on her computer. Joan listened quietly to this shocking confession, and, being a compassionate type of person, and a loyal friend, was able to forgive Agnes all her bad deeds, and now she and Agnes are the best of friends again.

For her part, Agnes now feels certain that Hell is a reality and that the Devil really does exist.

UNIDENTIFIED REMAINS

In November 1987, thirty-one people died in the King's Cross Underground Station blaze. All of the victims were identified – except for one badly charred corpse. The male body remained anonymous, referred to only as 'One Hundred and Fifteen' by the coroner, and no relatives or friends came forward to put a name to the remains. It seemed probable that the body belonged to one of the many people in London who live rough and seek the warmth and shelter of the underground.

Over sixteen years elapsed until January 2004, when forensic experts from the British Transport Police finally concluded that 'One Hundred and Fifteen' had been a seventy-two-year-old man from Scotland by the name of Alexander Fallon. After the death of his wife from ovarian cancer in 1974, Alexander Fallon had gone to pieces, eventually selling up his house in Falkirk and moving to London in the early 1980s, where he ended up living rough on the streets. At last, the mystery of Mr One Hundred and Fifteen had been solved.

Further back in time, another railway disaster created a similar mystery, but this puzzle has never been solved, though there are tantalising clues that may one day provide a solution.

It all began in the dark foggy hours of the Saturday morning of 13 October, 1928. At 4.28am, the Leeds to Bristol night mail steamed at a steady sixty miles per hour through dense fog and collided with a train that was being shunted on to a station siding. The mail train was thrown by the impact into the path of an oncoming freight train. In those days, railway carriages were gas-lit, and the cylinders of gas onboard the train exploded on impact, creating a raging inferno which tore through the carriages.

This nightmare scenario took place under the road bridge at Charfield Station, twenty miles south of Gloucester. A handful of locals who were out at that early predawn hour witnessed some amazing and terrifying sights. One sleeping passenger on the hellbound train had been awakened by the almighty crash, and had managed to stumble out of the door of his carriage, which was standing on its end. By pure luck, he stepped out from the train, directly on to the humped-back bridge above it, and he kept on walking, obviously in a state of shock, never to return. Another man was wandering around in a daze, screaming out through the choking clouds and searing flames for the girl he was due to marry soon. All he was ever able to find of her was her handbag.

Some were lucky that morning, others weren't. The dreadful aroma of burning flesh, and the screams of the passengers trapped in their blazing carriages, horrified onlookers and would haunt the memories of the survivors for years to come. One rescuer broke down and cried when he heard the agonised pleas of a group of survivors pinned under a blazing carriage, begging for someone to cut off their legs, to free them from the blistering heat. Another man had to be punched unconscious because he refused to leave his trapped sister to die in the fire-gutted wreckage. She pleaded for help from him, and when he regained consciousness he could still hear her terrible screams.

What little remained of the Charfield disaster victims was very difficult to identify, and many relatives of those still missing accepted the railway company's offer to bury what was left of their loved ones in a mass grave in the village churchyard. Upon the memorial stone of that grave, ten names are inscribed, and at the bottom of the list are the words: 'Two Unknown'. The two unidentified bodies from the three-train pile-up had apparently been those of a boy of eleven or twelve, and a girl aged about nine, and, amazingly, no one had come forward to identify them. It is one thing for an old man to have no one in the world who cares about him, but quite another for two children to be burned to death and no one to miss them.

In the seventy-six years that have elapsed since the Charfield tragedy, the two forgotten children remain nameless and unclaimed. A porter on the doomed train named Haines distinctly remembered two schoolchildren being on the train at Gloucester station that fateful morning. Haines had moved along the train checking tickets, and had found the boy and girl travelling alone and overnight, a curious state of affairs, which fixed the sighting in the porter's memory. The children had their own tickets, and each had been wearing a school cap of some kind. Police Sergeant Crook later stated that part of a school blazer found among the crash debris, was of a size to fit a boy or girl aged between eight and ten, and had been an Air Force blue colour with black ribbon around the pockets. On the blazer was a distinctive badge with a floral design on a red background, and it bore the motto, 'Luce Magistra', which, when translated, means, 'By Light, Mistress'.

Despite these very specific clues and a nationwide publicity campaign via the national newspapers, no school in Britain came forward to claim the pupils, or to identify the badge and blazer. Neither did any parents or guardians come forward seeking their missing children, and therein lies the mystery of the forgotten railway children. Official and amateur detectives across the land tried to connect the blazer and badge with a school, but were unsuccessful, so it was assumed that the two mysterious children must have been educated abroad.

However, I researched this fascinating case many years ago and discovered that the Air Force blue blazer and it's Luce Magistra badge was worn – and still is worn – by the pupils of Queen Ethelburga's private boarding school near Harrogate. The ill-fated train on which the unknown children were travelling, was running from Leeds, which is very near to Queen Ethelburga's, yet neither the headmistress of the time, nor any of the school's teachers, contacted the authorities to identify the blazer and it's unique motto. This raises the possibility that the children were on the run from some kind of mental or physical abuse. But even if that was the case, how come they were never missed by their parents, friends and relatives? Perhaps they had uncovered some far-reaching scandal and had been fleeing to the safety of their parents' home by train. The possibilities are endless.

According to some of the Charfield locals, a mysterious woman in black was often seen visiting the grave of the two unknowns from 1929 to the 1950s. She used to step out of a chauffeur-driven limousine of German make, and then spend a long time staring at the memorial stone on the Charfield train crash victims' grave.

Does this have any bearing on the riddle of the forgotten railway children? And what has this intriguing story got to do with Liverpool hauntings? Well, on three separate occasions in October 1979, a Liverpool man named Tony O'Neil was visiting relatives in Cheltenham, and he certainly knew nothing about the Charfield train crash of 1928.

One evening, around 9.15pm, Mr O'Neil looked up from his newspaper, and was amazed to suddenly see a boy of about fourteen and a girl of around seven or eight years of age sitting on the opposite side of the carriage. The seats which the youngsters occupied had been vacant just seconds before. Mr O'Neil noted that the boy was wearing a dark blue school cap and uniform, and held a satchel on his knee. The girl was partly obscured by the boy, but she too wore a similar uniform. The boy turned towards Mr O'Neil with a sad expression on his face, then instantly vanished, along with the girl.

Tony O'Neil witnessed the appearance and dematerialisation of the same boy and girl on the train to Cheltenham at the very same time on two more occasions, and on 13 October – the anniversary of the Charfield crash of 1928 – the ghosts were not only seen by O'Neil but also by a woman passenger who let out a scream. Although the woman was shocked by the phantom schoolchildren, she noted that their reflections in the carriage window disappeared along with them too, as if they had been physically real. A railway ticket inspector at Cheltenham later told Mr O'Neil and the female passenger that the spectral schoolchildren had been seen on the train on many occasions.

Are the apparitions of the sorrowful-looking duo the earthbound spirits of Charfield's 'two unknown'? Perhaps they will continue to haunt the modern trains bound for Cheltenham until such time as we uncover their true identities and determine why they were travelling unsupervised on the train bound for nowhere.

SAVED BY A BEE

In the first edition of *Haunted Liverpool 8*, I introduced readers to an amateur Victorian sleuth, Mrs Gloria Hamlet, and her trusty side-kick, Florrie Perkins, who, between them, tackled many intriguing crimes. After being widowed at the age of twenty-nine, Mrs Hamlet left her Cheshire home and came to Liverpool, where she set up a small chandler's shop in Bold Street. Florrie helped in the shop, as well as delivering purchases to customers' homes on her bicycle. Mrs Hamlet and Florrie Perkins obviously loved the challenge of solving local mysteries, amongst them the following bizarre tale.

One beautiful sunny evening in June 1881, at precisely 7pm, a thirty-one-year-old mathematics tutor, Lawrence Williams, was leaning out of the window of his top-floor lodgings, enjoying the view and smoking his pipe. As he puffed away, idly watching the people and carriages passing by below on Clarence Street – a huge bumble bee came buzzing through the air directly towards him. Williams batted the bee away with his pipe – and at precisely the same time, there was a loud bang in the street. A bullet whizzed past the maths teacher's head, grazing his cheek and shattering the mirror on his dresser. Williams dived for cover, and when his landlady Mrs Bronte came rushing into the room, Williams screamed at her to stay away from the window and dive for cover.

There were no more shots, and the police were soon on the scene. The bullet had been of a .44 calibre, and one detective thought the Fenians – an Irish terrorist group – could be behind the shooting. Only a week earlier the Irishmen had attempted to dynamite Liverpool Town Hall for their cause: home rule for Ireland. The houses on the other side of

Clarence Street were searched, but no trace of any gunman was found, although they did uncover one possible lead, but the police didn't pursue it as thoroughly as they might have.

The window in a lodging house facing Williams's room had been left open, and the lodger – a Mr Sylvester – hadn't been seen since he left at eight o'clock that morning. His room was checked, and although a faint aroma of cordite hung in the air, no gun was found. The landlord said that Sylvester had paid a month's rent in advance. He had been a very, very small, quiet, inoffensive-looking man, yet other lodgers claimed that the gunshot had definitely originated in his room. Nothing seemed to add up, as Sylvester's room had been empty and locked at the time of the shooting, and no one was seen or heard to run from it. The landlord had rushed upstairs immediately after hearing the tremendous bang, and no one had passed him on his way up. If the gunshot had indeed come from that room, then the gunman must have been invisible.

Detectives then asked Williams if he knew of anyone who would want to harm him. The teacher thought long and hard, but couldn't think of anyone who might have a grudge against him. The strange incident was gradually forgotten, the police having decided that the whole thing had been an accidental shooting by someone messing about with a pistol, which did not warrant further investigation.

Mrs Gloria Hamlet, however, was not one to let a mystery rest and became fascinated by the incident. She not only interviewed Williams, but also visited the lodging house where the mysterious would-be assassin was thought to have had a room. The landlord took a liking to the attractive-looking detective, and upon her second visit to the lodging house he admitted – over a glass of sherry – that he had found two objects in the room which had been abandoned by the mysterious Mr Sylvester: a book of illustrated nursery rhymes, left open at a certain page, and a beautiful, expensive-looking clock. Mrs Hamlet inspected the clock, which was a French Japy Frères model, eighteen inches in height – not the sort of item a person would overlook, even if they were leaving in a hurry. The purple ribbon in the book of nursery rhymes had been left in the page that displayed the following verse:

> *There was a little man and he had a little gun,*
> *And his bullets were made of lead, lead, lead;*
> *He went to the brook, and shot a little duck,*
> *Right through the middle of its head, head, head.*

Perhaps the rhyme contained some kind of clue, Mrs Hamlet mused. She examined the clock, and noticed that the silver medallion on its front slid sideways. She then gazed through a hole in the back of the timepiece – and was shocked to discover that she was looking through a cross-haired gun-sight. The clock was carefully dismantled, and found to contain a .44 percussion revolver, with its trigger tied to a lever amongst the timepiece's cogs. The clock had been set up to fire the gun at 7pm – long after Mr Sylvester had left his lodgings for good.

The intended victim – Mr Williams – shuddered when he was told of Mrs Hamlet's findings, and he suddenly remembered the comical-looking 'midget' whom he and a friend had made fun of some three weeks before the shooting. They had belly-laughed at the diminutive man as he passed below the window. The teacher and his friend had been drinking and were quite tipsy that evening.

Williams was an idiosyncratic man of habit, and each evening, at precisely 7pm, he could be seen smoking his pipe at his window. The little man must have noticed this and, inwardly seething because of Williams's insensitive behaviour, had plotted his ingenious revenge. It could have been the perfect murder, had the bullet struck its target squarely. Instead, a humble bumble bee had saved the life of Lawrence Williams.

Mr Sylvester was never traced. He was undoubtedly a warped genius, and I have the unsettling feeling that he may have actually killed before, and after, the mysterious Clarence Street shooting. Perhaps his murders were executed so cleverly, that they were made to look like accidents.

An example of such a crime that comes to mind, was the discovery of a mysterious copper pipe that was found plumbed into the Corporation Baths in Archer Street, Kirkdale, in 1882. The pipe had been lethally linked to a lightning conductor with the undisguised intention of causing major harm. The pipe was quickly removed, and just who put it there remains a mystery. Had there been a lightning strike upon the conductor, many people in contact with water from the pipes would have been killed.

WHO GOES THERE?

I once read a yellowed, time-worn letter from a Mr R Gaskell of Stanhope Street, to Sir William Nott-Bower, Head Constable of Liverpool during the period 1881-1902. The letter was dated Saturday, 12 August 1899, and it related an intriguing story that blends crime and the supernatural. The contents of that letter, and further research of my own into its claims, have produced the following strange story.

In the Lancashire of the late nineteenth century, the name of a mysterious character in the underworld was tantalisingly heard time and time again, yet we know nothing about this person's background today, and the Victorian police were evidently none the wiser either. The name was Specolli and he seems to have been an elusive kingpin of crime in the days of Queen Victoria.

Specolli was rarely involved in crime directly, but seems to have had a league of lackeys and scoundrels at his disposal to carry out his ill-intentioned schemes. Specolli must have exercised a considerable power over his shady subjects in his dark realm of crime, as hardly any of them ever informed on him. Two that did were quickly silenced: one was found at the bottom of a dry dock with his head caved in, and the other was found hanged in the garret of his own home. His killing was made to look like suicide, with a note left at the scene of the hanging, even though the dead man was illiterate, unable to write even his own name. Specolli's tentacles reached all four corners of the county, but especially Liverpool, where he was thought to be living, not far from the old Chinatown quarter.

In 1886, rumours began to circulate about the 'Aladdins Cave' of an eccentric old man named James Grundy of Cornwallis Street. All that was known – and is still known to this day – was that Grundy had a horde of gold, money, jewellery, works of art, bric-a-brac, and other valuable items in his cellar, which was cordoned off from the coal cellar by a partition wall of granite. He had reams of inventory papers that listed the items of treasure, and those papers came into the hands of Mr Gaskell who first alerted me to this peculiar case.

The wealthy, but mentally unhealthy, Grundy, would prowl the alleyways at night, delving into dustbins and picking through midden heaps for scraps of food. Occasionally he would even resort to begging to sustain himself, anything rather than dipping into his fortune. Despite his attempts to keep his fortune secret, somehow, somebody found out about it, and the whispers and rumours rippled across Liverpool and eventually reached the ears of Mr Specolli.

Specolli's first reaction was to try and put the rival criminals of the region off the scent by spreading a rumour about a quantity of gold bullion being temporarily stored in a dock warehouse in the north of Liverpool. Specolli even sent a bogus tip-off letter to a major criminal in the form of a business proposal. Under the name Williams, he stated that he had been unfairly sacked by a certain bank and now wished to exact his revenge on his former employees by providing inside information on the security procedures at the warehouse, in return for reasonable remuneration.

As the rival crooks of the city were occupied with the bogus proposal, Specolli sent his spies out to Cornwallis Street to watch over Grundy's house, and they gleefully noted that the old man had not even taken the precaution of adding secure locks to his doors, or bars to his windows. The spies reported back to Specolli, and he mentally drew up the plan to steal the treasure from the cellar strong-room.

Specolli's supreme lock-picker, a man named Crilly, and a brute nicknamed 'Tubby' Rogers, would enter the premises with Grundy at night when the rich old eccentric had returned from his scavenging. They would then force him to open the vault, after which Tubby would keep him downstairs and bind and gag him. Crilly would go to the drawing room window of the house and give a signal to a third accomplice, and he in turn would light his pipe, to signal to the four-wheeled 'growler' coach waiting on the corner, in the shadows of St Michael's graveyard. That coach would call at Grundy's home and transport the valuables to a half-way house on Harrowby Street, three quarters of a mile away. The loot would be divided and taken to five separate locations, to be left there until the heat died down.

This is where the story takes a turn into the uncanny. Specolli's carefully thought-out plan went smoothly and James Grundy was parted from his long-hoarded treasure. For safety, the booty was hidden in different locations, and one fifth of it was sent to the cellar of a house in Anfield. In the seclusion of the cellar the haul was examined, and amongst it there was a small wooden chest, about two feet in height and five feet in length. It was secured by several large padlocks. Upon the lid of the chest, a small silver crucifix was stapled with strips of green-tinted copper. In faded chalk, the three words 'from the *Amity*' had been scrawled on the side of the chest.

The thieves were naturally impatient to discover what was contained in the securely-bound chest, but not having the expert lock-picker Mr Crilly at hand, they decided to use hammers and chisels instead. When the lid was prised off that chest, an icy·draft blew out of its interior, and the sound of laughter echoed throughout the cellar. Specolli's two lackeys were thrown about by an immensely powerful force. As soon as they had regained their footing, they ran out of the cellar, and as they dashed to the front door, the sound of heavy running footsteps pursued them. For several streets the invisible pursuer kept up the chase, until the eerie footsteps faded away. Crilly and Rogers were so terrified by the supernatural incident, that they refused to return to the cellar until daybreak.

By the time the thieves conjured up enough courage to go back to the house, the loot had been stolen, probably by some chancer who had wandered into the house after seeing the front door standing ajar. The police investigated the robbery at James Grundy's house and a few minor arrests were subsequently made, but, as usual, Specolli – the mastermind behind the whole thing – escaped, and the other four fifths of the loot from Grundy's cellar was never recovered.

Decades later, it was rumoured that Specolli had given himself a new identity and gone to live on the Isle of Man to escape several violent members of his own family, who were thought to be recent Italian immigrants. Specolli was said to be easily recognisable to the police because he had a prominent black mark under his left eye – apparently the scar left by an adder bite sustained in childhood. Despite this, Specolli vanished into obscurity.

The intriguing part of the tale concerning Grundy is the sinister wooden chest from the *Amity* stored in his cellar with a crucifix stapled to it. The sailing ship the *Amity* was built at New York in 1816 and she served the Black Ball Line of sailing packets between New York and Liverpool until 1824, when she was wrecked on Squam Beach, New Jersey. The *Amity* was one hundred and six feet and six inches in length, with a beam of twenty-eight feet and a hold over fourteen feet deep. She once made a crossing between Liverpool and New York in just twenty-two days, yet this fast and reliable ship had acquired quite a sinister reputation. It was claimed that she was harbouring something supernatural that few superstitious Jack Tars in New York or Liverpool were prepared to even talk about, for fear of incurring forces that cannot yet be comprehended by mortals.

In the 1820s these weird rumours about the *Amity* were seemingly confirmed when the ship arrived at Liverpool Docks from Rexton, New Brunswick, after a voyage of twenty-eight days. Beneath the casks which made up most of the cargo, in the floor of the hold, the body of a partially decomposed man was discovered. His off-white eyes bulged obscenely out of their sockets and his emaciated face, though discoloured and shrunken, still wore an expression of raw terror. It seemed as if he had died from fright, as the coroner was unable to determine the cause of death.

Rumours were rife and swept through the Liverpool docks like an ill wind. Some said the body was that of a deserter who had hidden in the *Amity's* hold, but enquiries by the Canadian police at Brunswick disproved this, and the corpse was never identified.

Crew from the *Amity*, most of them unaware of the grisly discovery in the hold, gathered in the waterfront taverns of Liverpool and whispered about the nerve-wracking 'thing' that haunted their ship during its recent voyage. It had all started some months back when the *Amity* was locked in ice in the Canadian harbour of Richibucto. The cold that winter was so severe, that a crewman lost his nose to frostbite, and ship hands risked losing their fingers as they handled the ship's rigging which was permanently coated with a thick layer of snow and ice. As temperatures continued to plummet, the captain and crew were forced to take temporary refuge inside the stricken ship, where they huddled together supping extra tots of rum and whiskey to ward off the intense cold. Even down in the cabins they could still see their breath and could not sleep because of the cold.

At three in the morning, the officer of the watch blew furiously on his frozen fingers and stamped his feet in an effort to keep out the cold and was counting the minutes to the end of his watch, when he heard the sound of someone, or something, treading on the creaking sheet ice, which had the ship in its vice-like grip. He looked over the rail and saw nothing but a low sea mist suspended in a layer across the frozen waters. He spat overboard nervously and the saliva instantly turned into crystals, stinging his already chapped lips. Later that morning, the crew not only heard the sounds of someone walking through the ship's hold, they also claimed to be startled by the pale misty exhalations of breath from something that was invisible to their eyes.

The ghostly entity then made itself scarce for a week, but when the *Amity* finally broke free from the ice, 'the Invisible' as the First Mate called the phantom, suddenly became very active once again. The captain tried to calm the nerves of his terrified crew by claiming, rather lamely, that the ghost was nothing more than the sounds of the ship's timbers settling back into place after their long exposure to the sub-zero temperatures. All the same, the captain slept with a lamp at his bedside and with the ship's Bible within easy reach. The Invisible allegedly materialised from time to time during the voyage to Liverpool, and when it did so, the sight was so shocking, that one old sailor almost died from heart failure. The descriptions of the entity varied from "a fiend that looked like Old Nick himself" to "a slimy, lizard-skinned devil".

Whatever the thing on board the *Amity* was, it seems to have departed the ship at Liverpool Docks, for the ship's crew never experienced another paranormal incident after that voyage was completed. The identity of the dead man found in the *Amity's* hold was never determined, and so we must assume that he was a stowaway, who had perhaps died from starvation, dehydration or hypothermia. Or perhaps the 'thing' literally scared him to death.

All of this makes me wonder if some skilled occultist or exorcist managed to contain the ghostlike being from the *Amity* and imprison it in the locked chest with the crucifix attached to it. How and why James Grundy had come into possession of the chest is another mystery. If Specolli's cronies unwittingly released the invisible creature, what became of it? Scarier still, could it still be at large?

DEATH WAS A STRANGER

One of the most curious stories I have looked into began one morning on a certain Liverpool street in the summer of 1997. A thin gangly man, aged about thirty, with long greasy hair, a faded blue tee shirt, stained jeans and grimy scuffed tennis shoes, came slowly down the street. His stubbled face was turned down to the pavement and he seemed to be so engrossed in his own sad thoughts that he was unaware of anything else around him. Tracking him at a walking pace, came a black BMW, cruising down the street a few yards behind him. In the car were three shaven-headed men, all in their twenties, and all wearing expensive, brand new track suits and immaculate, costly trainers. The windows were wound down and the skinheads surveyed the scruffily-dressed pedestrian with unpleasant smirks on their overly-tanned faces. The driver, in his designer shades, glanced back and forth between the street and the scruffy man.

Minutes later, the BMW rolled to a halt outside the large house where the three skinheads lived and worked. Their occupations lay in the criminal sphere. They committed burglaries on a regular basis and supplemented their income, whenever it was necessary, by distributing a variety of drugs to the neighbourhood junkies. However, in recent months, the trio had been forced to suspend their drug-pushing activities because a determined team of narcotics officers had been repeatedly raiding suspect premises in the area. We'll call the three shaven-headed n'er-do-wells Lee, Paul and Jason – not their real names.

The three of them sprang out of the BMW and jokingly seized the dishevelled man and jostled him towards the house. He meekly protested as two of the skinheads manhandled him down the hallway, through the back-kitchen, and out into the sunny back yard. The eldest of the criminals, Lee, went upstairs and returned shortly afterwards brandishing a pair of electric hair clippers, with no comb attachment fitted.

Jason and Paul roughly removed the stranger's clothes and when he pulled away and raised his voice in protest, they slapped his face and told him to shut up. Every item of clothing, including his dirty underwear, was removed from 'the hippy', as they now decided to call him, and Jason proceeded to shave off the poor man's hair with the clippers. The transformation from dishevelled, grubby, oily-haired beatnik into a streamlined hygienic skinhead was almost complete. The man was bundled into an almost unbearably hot shower and scrubbed by six hands. Afterwards, the stranger was shaved, and Hugo Boss cologne was slapped into his face, which was speckled with shaving cuts. The former drop-out was treated to some Calvin Klein underwear and a smart tracksuit from Wade Smith.

The newly groomed guest was thankful but had severe doubts about their motives and was quite anxious to leave the house, but Lee, Jason and Paul told him to relax and sat him at a table where one of them laid a thin line of coke.

"What's your name, mate?" Lee asked, putting his arm around the unknown man.

"John," came the reply.

"Well, John, have some whiz."

Lee pushed John's face down towards the line of white powder. "No, I'm sorry, but I'm not into drugs," John mumbled, apologetically.

"Are you a retard?" Jason asked, seriously. He thought John's apparent slowness of mind and clumsy actions belied some kind of mental problem.

Lee's temper flared. He was a very muscular man and he grabbed John's arm and yanked it up his back, then pushed his face into the coke powder. John groaned – then puffed and blew away the powder, which provoked a beating from all three. He was bundled into a spare room in the house and kept there under lock and key. John tried to shout for help but his captors would blast music as loud as they could from a CD player to blot out the noise. The neighbours were so afraid of the drug dealers, that they never complained to them, or the police.

Three days later, John was still being held captive at the house, when he was escorted downstairs to a back room where Lee, Paul and Jason were smoking marijuana. It was eleven o'clock in the evening and the vertical blinds were open, admitting silver stripes of moonlight from a full summer moon. A radio was whispering on low volume, and a crimson lava lamp undulated hypnotically on the mantelpiece.

John was pushed into a deep leather armchair, while Lee sprawled out on a sofa, and talked about feeling tranquil, and Paul and Jason sat on the floor, gazing up at a tank of tropical fish on the sideboard. John refused to smoke any pot, but Lee was so drugged, that this time he took no offence and accepted his captive's refusal. As the night wore on, the skinheads lost all sense of time, and the drug seemed to remove the false personas of the street-hard tough-guys.

"Wonder if a swan can break your arm, just by flapping its wing," Lee suddenly mused, and started to giggle, thinking about the way his father would warn him not to go near the swans on Sefton Park's boating lake when he was a boy.

"Wonder why the moon's round and not square," Paul idly remarked, watching the moon sinking ever so slowly beyond the silhouetted rooftops.

Jason exhaled a perfect smoke ring from his rolled-up joint and murmured, "Round is natural."

All the external doors were locked, and so John was allowed to make himself a cup of tea in the kitchen. The effects of the drug and the mellowness of the summer evening were conducive to an unexpected mystical discussion about life after death among the criminals. "I reckon there's something after this, deffo," Jason said, staring at the luminescent graphic equaliser display on the radio.

"Yeah, a six foot hole," was Lee's response.

"Yeah, but say you get cremated?" Paul asked.

"Okay, then, there's just an urnful of ashes ... a mixture of other people's ashes mixed in as well probably."

"What d'you mean?" Jason asked.

"I heard that they save a few bob by cremating a few bodies at once," Lee told him with a smirk.

"That's well out of order," Jason protested.

The subject turned to ghost stories, and each of the skinheads told a supernatural tale, then they asked John if he knew any ghost stories. He shook his head, then added, "But lot of strange things have happened to me though."

"What like?" Lee said, suddenly propping himself up on one arm and taking an interest. He rested on his stomach, then focused his attention on the abducted 'guest'.

"People around me always die," said John, flatly.

At that moment, Lee, Paul and Jason felt a sudden cold current of air from the open window brush against the back of their necks.

"How d'you mean, 'always die'?" asked Lee.

"I've lost my entire family to accidents, to cancer, to suicides. I've had five girlfriends in my life and they've all died within months of my meeting them. I'm like the angel of death. Like a fatal jinx on everybody I meet."

"Maybe you're just unlucky," Jason said, after a long tense pause.

"No, it's more than that," John insisted, "I'm like the Grim Reaper, and I don't know why. When I was young I was put in one school after another. Teachers died in fires, car crashes … friends I made choked on sweets, were murdered, or knocked down … the schools would change, but the outcome was always the same. It's gone on and on and I'm so tired of it. Behind me there's a trail of dead bodies."

"No way!" Lee said, and, he saw how nervous Jason and Paul seemed all of a sudden.

That night, when John was put back in his room, the skinheads argued amongst themselves. "I'll let him go in a few days. I'm just hanging on to him for a laugh," Lee explained to his younger accomplices.

"There's something not right about him, Lee," Jason said. "He gives me the creeps."

"Just let him go now," Paul suggested. "What's the point of keeping him?"

"You big soft tart," said Lee. "In a few days we'll let him go. He's just a weirdo. Now get to bed."

On the following morning, Jason was in the shower, when he felt a hard, round lump under his armpit. It was not at all painful, but it was very definitely a lump, and he panicked. He told his mates about it as they ate their cornflakes, trying not to sound as if he was scared. Paul advised him to go to the doctor's straight away, but Lee dismissed the lump, saying it was probably just an overactive sweat gland.

Later that day, there was a frantic knocking at the door. It was Lee's mother, and she was in floods of tears. Her brother, Lee's uncle, had just died. Lee's dad had died when he was a child and his Uncle David had raised him like a father. Lee's mother said she had found her brother hanging out of his bed, clutching his chest and gasping for breath. He had begged her to call an ambulance, but died from what looked like a heart attack before she could even get to the telephone. During the confusion, as Lee rushed to his mother's home, John slipped out of the house and back into the obscurity of the street.

Within a week, Paul was dead from an accidental heroin overdose. His blue bloated body had lain decomposing in the shared house while Lee stayed a week with his grief-stricken mother. When he found Paul's corpse, it was covered in maggots and bluebottles.

Jason did go to the doctors with his lump and was quickly diagnosed with cancer. He was sent to Clatterbridge Hospital to undergo a programme of intense chemotherapy.

A month later, Lee's mother was deserted by her lover of six years, and that, coupled with the traumatic loss of her brother, caused her to suffer a nervous breakdown which resulted in her needing treatment in a psychiatric hospital.

From Clatterbridge, Jason wrote to me about these tragic incidents, and the claims of the mysterious John. Jason was convinced that John was some kind of harbinger of death, and sadly, months after writing the letter, he lost his battle against cancer.

In 1999, Lee committed suicide by attaching a pipe to his car exhaust and feeding it into his BMW in a garage at a house in Brighton. At the time of his death, there were rumours that he had recently been diagnosed with AIDs.

Was the spate of deaths nothing more than a cluster of dark coincidences? Or did the weird stranger actually cast a shadow of death on his captors?

THE CANNIBAL

I uncovered this gruesome spine-tingler in an article which I found in the nineteenth century newspaper, the *Liverpool Albion* and a short version of the story has appeared in one of my earlier books, but here it is again in all its grisly detail.

In July 1884, a cargo-carrying brigantine called the *Pierrot* set sail from Montevideo for the port of Liverpool. She was a large vessel: one hundred and ten feet long and thirty feet across the beam. She weighed two hundred and eighty-two tons. The ship was under the command of a seasoned old Liverpool captain, Edward Grace, a man who was renowned in the city's maritime community as a sinister eccentric. Grace was known to be a member of a bizarre club in London known as the Society for the Acclimatisation of Animals in the United Kingdom; an organisation devoted to increasing the nation's food supply by breeding exotic creatures, from kangaroos to bison, in the fields of England.

The founder of this fellowship of crackpots was Captain Grace's friend, Francis Buckland, a wealthy surgeon and eminent naturalist. Buckland was notorious for eating such dubious delicacies as boiled elephant trunk, mouse on toast and stewed mole garnished with blue bottles. On one occasion, Buckland and Grace allegedly even ate the preserved relic of a French monarch, Louis XIV, which had been plundered from the royal tomb during the French Revolution. Buckland and Grace did not suffer from the slightest trace of indigestion after this repellant feast, and both agreed that the heart had tasted much better when eaten with gravy made from the blood of a marmoset monkey.

Only two members of the *Pierrot's* crew of nine knew about their captain's perverted appetite. They were First Mate, Jack

Burbage and Second Mate, Albert Cribbin, who both found Grace to be a repulsive and domineering man and had vowed never to serve under his command again after the Montevideo voyage was completed. However, in mid-Atlantic, the *Pierrot* ran into a violent storm, and was blown into an uncharted rock, creating a thirty-foot gash in the brigantine's hull. The ship's hold rapidly started to fill with water.

As if this state of affairs were not dire enough, an enormous wave then swamped the stricken vessel and swept five crewmen over board. Captain Grace and the four surviving crew members managed to launch the life boat and proceeded to row away as rapidly as they could from the rapidly sinking ship, before the suction could drag them all down with it. As they rowed furiously away, they heard a desperate voice shouting to them. The old cook stopped rowing and pointed to a head, bobbing up and down next to the lifeboat. "It's the purser, Mr King!" he cried.

Captain Grace uttered a stream of profanities then said, "He's damned! Leave him. Save yourselves."

"We can't just leave him to die, sir," pleaded the sixteen-year-old cabin boy, Richard Tomlin, who had also stopped rowing.

The other two rowers in the boat, the First and Second Mates, were also regarding the drowning purser sympathetically. Knowing he was risking the Captain's wrath, the old cook let go of his oar and, leaning over the side of the boat, reached out towards the purser saying, "Quick, jump in."

Again Captain Grace shouted, "He'll capsize us! Let him be."

The cook took no heed of Grace's warning, so the Captain grabbed the elderly man's oar and lifted it high above him. The three other survivors watched, speechless with shock, as Grace brought it down on the cook's head, smashing his skull like an eggshell. The sickening impact sent blood spraying out of his ears and the old man toppled overboard into the sea. The abandoned purser swore at the Captain and latched on to the corpse in a vain attempt to stay afloat. Grace then turned to the other survivors, still wielding the oar in a threatening manner. "Row this boat from here right now, or you'll follow him!" he warned grimly.

The trembling cabin boy Tomlin, and the two other men, did as he said, and by some miracle, the boat survived the storm. Then the real hardship began. The lifeboat drifted aimlessly upon the vast expanses of ocean, under a bleaching blistering sun by day and through the biting cold of the night. The survivors were soon crazy with thirst, but they had no water to quench their parched, dust-dry throats. They tried gargling with salt water, which only made them vomit, and stung their blistered lips. They were soon suffering from heatstroke, dehydration and starvation. Day after long day they scanned the horizon for ships, or what would have been an even more welcome sight, the coastline, but they saw nothing other than bobbing waves as far as their tired eyes could see.

By the fifth day, the survivors were too weak to row for more than a few minutes at a stretch, and it seemed to be only a matter of time before they died, one by one, of thirst and starvation. But the ever-resourceful Captain Grace had a suggestion – a suggestion so horrible that it sent shivers down the spines of the two officers and the cabin boy. He coughed to clear his dried up throat and in a gruff, parched voice announced, "There's only one alternative left to us. We draw lots, and the unlucky one gets eaten." The First Mate flinched in horrified disbelief and shook his head vigorously. Undeterred, Captain Grace opened the lifeboat's small medicine box. All it contained was a roll of bandage, a small phial of iodine, and a needle and thread. He suggested cutting four lengths of bandage. The one who chose the shortest would be killed to feed the other three.

"No, Captain! Someone will pick us up soon, " argued the Second Mate. "It can't be long now. A ship's bound to pass us soon."

Grace ignored him and took out his clasp knife. "It's the only way we can survive. We eat animals, don't we? Well, a man is just an animal too. They do it in the Polynesian Islands."

"It's three against one, sir," said the First Mate, picking up the oar, ready to hit the Captain with it if necessary.

Grace smiled, then put the knife back in its sheath and said, "You're right. I can see I'm outnumbered," and he closed his eyes and pretended to doze off.

In the golden rays of the following morning's sunshine, the First and Second Mate awoke from a fitful night's sleep to a hellish scene. The Captain's mouth was dripping with blood and they realised that he was in the process of breakfasting off the cabin boy, Richard Tomlin. He had evidently slit the poor lad's throat during the night, probably while he was sleeping, and was now carving the flesh from his forearm with the clasp knife. The ravenous villain made vile slurping noises as he ate, and seemed unaware that he was being watched by the other two. Fearing that he might be next, the First Mate, Jack Burbage, picked up the heavy oar and struck the cannibalistic Captain across the head with it. The blow sent Grace reeling across the boat, and he came to rest on his back, out cold.

The two officers stared in horror and disgust at the remains of slaughtered teenager, then Burbage picked up the captain's clasp knife and knelt down, ready to slit Grace's throat. The Second Mate managed to persuade his colleague not to commit murder, or it would look as if he had killed the cabin boy as well. When Grace regained consciousness, he saw the First Mate standing over him with the knife.

"I ... I only did it so we could survive," he stammered, seeing the murderous look on Burbage's face. "I ... I didn't want to kill the boy."

Over the next two days, the First and Second Mate had to take turns to sleep, because they couldn't trust the demented Captain Grace and they didn't want to end up like poor Tomlin. But through the combined effects of starvation and thirst, the officers became so weak that, in the end, they both collapsed, leaving them at the mercy of the Captain. Surprisingly, Grace didn't harm them; instead, he attempted to nurse them back to health by force feeding them with the cabin boy's flesh. To stop the skinned corpse from perishing in the noonday heat, he had dipped a roll of bandage from the medicine box in the seawater, then wrapped it around Tomlin's body.

Several days later, when all three men were close to death, a British naval vessel sighted their boat and came to their rescue. The sailors felt nauseous when they realised that the grotesque bundle lying in the bottom of the boat was actually the bandaged corpse of a boy; a corpse that was no longer intact. And when the sailors saw the streaks and smears of blood around the mouths of all three semi-conscious survivors, they soon put two and two together.

Captain Grace and his officers were taken to Portsmouth and charged with murder, but the Home Secretary thought the men had been through enough already, so he commuted their sentences to six months' hard labour at Dartmoor prison. When Grace had served his time, he changed his name and grew a beard before returning to Liverpool to look for work. He soon found employment as a stevedore, but the moment he was paid at the end of each week, he would squander his entire wages in the saloons of the Dock Road.

It was around this time that the hallucinations began. One night he saw the decomposing face of the cabin boy he had murdered, peering at him through the window of the Crow's Nest pub. Another time, Grace was staggering drunkenly down Paradise Street in a swirling fog, when he was confronted with the bandaged and bloodstained corpse of Richard Tomlin. The cabin boy, almost devoid of any skin and flesh, held his arms out to the terrified ex-captain and chased after him.

These hallucinations became steadily worse, and wherever Edward Grace ventured out in the city, the thing in bandages followed him. In the end, he ran into a police station in a frantic state and ranted about the awful revenge which Tomlin's ghost was exacting on him. Smelling the alcohol on his breath, the police surmised that the only spirits troubling the hysterical old man were those of the alcoholic kind, and they decided it would be in the public interest to throw him into a cell for the night. Accordingly, Grace was locked up in the Anfield Road Bridewell to sleep off the drink, but on the following morning, he was found dead in his cell by the officer on duty. The mariner's body was lying curled up under the iron bed, and his eyes were wide with terror. In Edward Grace's right hand, he was clutching a bloody strip of torn bandage …

THE GIANT SPECTRE

The following story, concerning the world of crime meeting the world of ghosts, is briefly referred to in an old Edwardian book called *Knaves and Crooks*, by Dudley Dunning, and takes place between Liverpool and London.

Close to Garlands, the flamboyant, hedonistic nightclub on Eberle Street, just a stone's throw away from Dale Street, and just a stone's throw back in time, there was once a Turkish Baths where many hard-worked Victorian gentlemen used to escape from the pressures of mental and physical toil in the elaborate marble pools, pore-cleansing steam clouds, piping hot water jets and cool drinking fountains.

Within this relaxing marble sanctuary of sweltering vapours, one rainy March afternoon in 1886, two sophisticated burglars were whispering ideas to each other for possible 'jobs' they had their sights on. John Lee Yates and William Pryde, both aged fifty-two, discussed attractive opportunities in their sphere of crime. Mr Pryde described his ingenious plans to remove priceless silverware from Knowsley Hall, and Mr Yates countered it with in-depth talk about a magpie's nest of jewellery and gold which, he had been reliably informed, was ripe for the taking at Gawthorpe Hall, the stately home of the Shuttleworths.

However, their entrepreneurial chit-chat was soon cut short by the speedy approach of the stout bath attendant. The flabby fellow handed Mr Pryde a sealed envelope with one hand, while wiping away the sweat which was permanently erupting on his forehead, with the other. He informed Mr Pryde that the letter had been given to him by a small round man in a pea-green suit outside the baths and that he had pressed it upon him in a most urgent manner. The description was immediately recognisable as 'Dicey' Devine, a small-time fence who often worked for Yates and Pryde.

Pryde tore open the envelope and read Dicey's distinctive handwriting, riddled, as usual, with appalling spelling mistakes. As he did so, an expression of shock passed across his flushed face. "Fingerspin is out," he said, and handed the note to Yates. Within minutes, Pryde and Yates were dried and dressed and were speeding in a hansom cab to their luxurious lodgings on Botanic Road in

Edge Hill, next to the park. They scurried up to their rooms, and there was Henry Player – expert lock-picker, pickpocket and cracksman extraordinaire, nicknamed 'Fingerspin' by his colleagues in the underworld.

He slouched back on the chaise longue lighting a Guinea Gold cigarette with a match, seemingly oblivious to the recent entry of Messrs Pryde and Yates.

The burglars bolted straight into the 'loot room' where their chests of swag were kept under lock and key, fully aware that the heavy padlocks on those chests would not have hindered Fingerspin in the least, should he have decided to take a look inside. He had been picking those types of locks, often in the pitch dark, since he was a kid. With great relief though, Pryde and Yates soon discovered that the chests were still full of booty. Their pickings and ill-gotten gains were intact. "I suppose it would be obtuse of me to ask how you gained access to this private apartment, Mr Player?" asked Yates, haughtily.

"Why, I let myself in, Mr Yates," was the offhand reply.

He rose from the chaise longue and silently circled round the shop window mannequin which was wearing a topper and a salt and pepper overcoat, which stood improbably in the corner. Pryde had been using the dummy to teach himself pickpocketing skills, without much success. Fingerspin nonchalantly brushed against the mannequin, and moments later, he presented the dummy's empty wallet to Yates and Pryde, as if he were displaying a winning poker hand. "What do you want with us?" Pryde asked, nervously re-checking the stash of silver in the chest.

Henry Player sat down again and told them he had just completed a five-year jail sentence for house-breaking. Now he was free, but stony broke. Managers of the shop, Lewis & Co, of Ranelagh Street – later destined to establish the famous Lewis's store – had been supplying free breakfasts to the unemployed for a month, and Henry had been very grateful for that morning meal, but now he wanted to live the high life once again, which would naturally necessitate resorting to a life of crime.

Henry Fingerspin Player then told his attentive listeners that those five long years in the cold Liverpool prison had been spent in the company of an old cockney named Nathan Yelski, who had been serving a ten-year sentence for defrauding a London bank. Yelski had been slowly dying from a consumptive disease, and Henry had looked after him well in the cell they shared. Yelski came to look upon Henry as a son, and Henry looked up to the old Hebrew as a fatherly figure.

Yelski's knowledge of locks was encyclopaedic, and he was also well acquainted with every loophole in English law. He would have made a first-class barrister, in fact, but had misused his brains and turned to crime instead. On many occasions, Yelski even managed to pick the lock of the cell-door, but he and Henry would never dare to venture out on to the prison landing for fear of harsh punishment and a sentence increase, and so the door would be locked again before the warders came along on their regular rounds.

Yelski was also gifted in the art of hypnosis, and the warders avoided looking him straight in the eye because of his mesmerising powers of suggestion. Weeks before the old man died, he revealed a marvellous secret to Henry, concerning the Bank of England. The secret was communicated to Yelski by an insider who had worked at the bank for many years.

Pryde and Yates sat on chairs opposite the released jailbird, hanging on to his every word, and carefully considering them with every swirl and winding ectoplasmic exhalation of Guinea Gold smoke. Fingerspin said that in 1836, the Directors of the Bank of England received an anonymous letter from someone who claimed to have access to their gold bullion store. The writer of the letter said that he could prove this by meeting them in the bullion vault at a pre-arranged hour. The directors concluded that the letter was the work of a hoaxer initially, but the staff at the bank took the letter's claims very seriously. The directors announced to the Press that they would wait in the bullion room on a certain night, and they actually went through with it. They assembled in the vault and waited with lanterns and pistols at the ready.

Sure enough, a scratching sound was heard in the bullion room that night, and the directors waited tensely for the cheeky bank robber to show himself. Presently, two floorboards on the cellar floor parted, and a head popped up. The head belonged to a man in his forties, although he was not a robber, but a sewerman. He'd been working in a sewer that ran under the celebrated bank, when he had noticed several bricks missing at the top of a drainage tunnel. The sewerman had then discovered, to his amazement, that directly above this tunnel was the bullion room of the Bank of England. On his first visit he had pushed the floorboards away and found himself among crate after crate of gold bars. The sewerman had refrained from committing any crime, and for his honesty, he was rewarded by the bank with a gift of eight hundred pounds.

However, that sewerman had a big mouth, and when he had been drinking a little too much Gold Watch in the local taverns, he would reveal, to anyone prepared to listen, the real reason behind his apparent honesty towards the 'Old Lady of Thread Needle Street'. He was terrified of the giant shadowy ghost that had attacked him when he made his first attempt to steal a box of gold bars. In most people, fear of the supernatural is greater than the desire for money, and this was certainly so in the case of the sewerman. He had scrambled from that bank and slipped head-first down into the murky stagnant waters of the sewer when the phantasm made a grab at him. Its fingers were long and grey – and icy, and they had grabbed at his neck as he was hanging the lantern over one of the bullion boxes. The thing had been at least seven feet in height, and its skeletal face was twisted with evil hatred as the sewerman reflexively held the lamp up to get a better look at it.

The old sewer worker had considered returning with a few of his friends for back-up, but that would have meant a share-out, and worse still, a mad gold rush to the vaults if they told their families. Then would surely come the risk of penal servitude. No, the shrewd sewerman decided that fake-honesty was the best policy, and so he had written anonymously to the bank authorities, offering to show them the vulnerable weak spot in their bullion room. As far as he was concerned, the more bankers who turned up in the vaults, the better, because the sewerman had no wish to meet that ghost on his own again.

Well, the bankers duly turned up and the sewerman rendezvoused with them, and thankfully no ghost materialised. He was well rewarded, but the money was gradually whittled away over the years, until the subterranean sanitation worker decided to take another look under the bank, and this time he went armed with a Bible and a silver crucifix, and was accompanied by his strong but slow-witted son.

On this occasion another branch of the sewer was discovered. This one was much smaller, and in a dangerous state of subsidence, and ran straight under the floor of the bullion room. The sewerman made a chaotic attempt at removing one of the bricks from the sewer's arched ceiling, and almost caused a cave-in. He retreated, fearing three things: being buried alive, arousing the unwanted attentions of the ghost and being heard by the people in the bank.

The sewer worker and his son therefore retreated, trudging their way through the dark labyrinth of brick-vaulted passages that spread for forty miles under the metropolis. The sewerman drew up a crude map of the sewage tunnel system beneath the Bank of England, and would often unfold it on the counter of the local tavern, before boring the drinkers and barflys with his daring schemes to enter the bullion rooms. All hot air of course, but one day, a young Nathan Yelski happened to see those plans, and bought them from the sewerman – with a forged banknote. Yelski later acquired the uniform of a sewerman – a blue smock, waterproof boots, and the slouch hat – then set off to survey the dangerous sewer.

In the dead of night, Yelski carefully prised open a manhole cover in a quiet street in the Old Jewry area of London, and gingerly ventured underground carrying a lantern. After quickly ascertaining that the sewer under the bank was in a perilously decrepit state, he turned around and went back the way he had come – all the time with a cold suspicion that he was being watched. Yelski was a secular materialist, with no interest in the world of spirits and superstition, but he had an overpowering feeling that the eyes of something were upon him when he was in the vicinity of the bank.

Yelski returned to his lodgings in the East End to mull things over. He decided that he would need specialised equipment and an accomplice to carry out the job, and in the meantime, he resorted to several frauds to keep the wolf from the door. For one of these frauds Yelski was arrested, tried and imprisoned, and during his incarceration, he shared a cell with a man named Sperry, who had worked as a cashier at the Bank of England – until he was caught selling quantities of the bank's special banknote paper to a group of forgers. Sperry told him that there was a reinforced safe in the bullion room of the Bank of England that contained the most priceless diamonds in the world.

One particular diamond in the safe which had remained in Sperry's memory, was the forty-four carat stone, the size of a large quail's egg, with two-hundred and six facets. It was a grade D, and of a flawless briolette cut. It was perfectly clear, and even when magnified twenty times, no fissures or imperfections were detectable. Because of the diamond's purity and uniqueness, it was valued at around £3 million. It was called the Paragon Diamond.

Sperry shocked Yelski when he said that he knew the combination to the diamond safe, but he would take the secret to the grave with him. Yelski promised that he would pay Sperry dearly for the secret of the combination once he was released in a year's time. Sperry belly-laughed at the offer.

Almost a week later, Yelski waited for the right moment, when he and Sperry were sitting on the bottom bunk in the cell, enjoying a brief game of cards before the lights went out. He gazed right into his cellmate's eyes and told him he looked fatigued. Sperry was soon caught by Yelski's hypnotic stare, and within minutes he was under the mesmeric spell. Within the short span of those minutes spent in a trance, Sperry revealed that the combination to the diamond safe was not a number at all. The safe was not unlocked by a single wheel, but by five small brass thumbwheels, each with letters on, and the letters that opened the safe spelt the word 'Simon' – the name of the Chief Cashier's cat.

Sperry gradually came out of the trance without realising that he had been hypnotised, thinking he'd been merely dozing, and unaware that he had revealed the most closely guarded secret of his life.

"Well, to cut a long story short," said Fingerspin, "Just

before Nathan Yelski died from consumption, he revealed the password to me and described the plan of the sewer under the Bank of England."

"That's a tall story if I ever heard one, Finger," sneered Pryde.

"Why are you telling us all of this?" Yates asked.

"I think we can pull it off between us, and then live like princes," Fingerspin said. "I can think of no two better accomplices."

"Rob the Old Lady? That's well out of our depth," gasped Pryde, "Jail's turned your mind."

Nevertheless, weeks later, at four in the morning, the three Liverpudlians blundered through a thick shroud of London fog, then stealthily descended into the stygian depths of the sewer system via a heavy, cast-iron manhole in the Old Jewery area of the capital. With each step, great brown sewer rats scampered away, as the three men slipped and slithered along the foul underground alleyways. They soon located the right sewer, and Pryde was immediately able to see the dangers at first-hand. He said it would be madness to risk a cave-in by removing bricks from the unsafe sewer to reach the bullion room – the whole lot could come down on top of them. Fingerspin carried a small pick and as he held the lantern up to inspect the loose, moss-covered bricks, he urged Pryde to reconsider, as they were all so near to an unimaginable fortune.

"It's suicide, Finger," Yates told him, "If that lot comes crashing down on us we'd be crushed before we had a chance to run. We need a supporting frame; a derrick ..."

"Think of that diamond ..." said Fingerspin, temptingly, "... the Paragon."

"We'd never reach it, Finger; not without specialist equipment. It's just too risky."

At that moment, Pryde turned, and saw something that left

him cold. On the walkway on the other side of the rushing channel of effluent – an abnormally tall black figure loomed, and it was watching them. It seemed to be about seven feet in height. Yates saw the giant silhouette too, and he and Pryde turned simultaneously to tell Fingerspin about the eerie watcher – when tragedy struck. Fingerspin, determined to get at the treasure, had levered loose a couple of bricks from the arched ceiling of the decaying sewer – and the bricks and clay they supported collapsed on top of him. The shadowy tall figure emitted a terrifying moaning sound and leapt straight across the channel and on to the walkway. Without a thought for Fingerspin, Pryde and Yates fought one another as they scurried away. Each looked back just once, and saw the sinister goliath hunched over the half-buried body of Henry Player.

When the two Liverpool cracksmen surfaced in the Old Jewry, they gasped and trembled in the foggy night air, then ran off through the ghostly vapours. They did not dare to go back to see if Fingerspin was dead or alive, for fear of being spotted by the police – and most importantly, for fear of encountering the inhuman thing that had appeared down there in subterranean London.

For years afterwards, John Lee Yates and William Pryde scanned the newspapers to see if the remains of Fingerspin had been discovered. Surely a sewerman would have come across the body? Or had the rats eaten the remains of their partner in crime? Not a word was ever published in the press to satisfy their grim curiosity.

However, on 2 August 1933, in a bizarre twist to the story, excavations were being carried out under the Bank of England, when a lead coffin, measuring seven feet and six inches in length was uncovered, at a depth of almost nine feet. The giant coffin bore a metal plate with the inscription: 'Mr William Daniel Jenkins. Died 24 March 1798, aged 31.' The skeletal body in the coffin measured six feet seven and a half inches – very tall by today's standards, but a veritable giant in those days. London historians soon carried out research, and it was discovered that the body was that of a Daniel Jenkins who had once been a clerk at the Bank of England. So the mysterious ghost in the sewers was probably his.

Some months before his death in 1798, Jenkins had undergone a dramatic change of character which had led some to think he had been possessed. He would scream and sob, and was convinced that he was about to die. He also confided to his family that he had a morbid fear that his body would be dissected by curious surgeons and put on display because of his abnormal height. The Bank of England arranged for Jenkins to be treated by its own doctors, and when their clerk passed away from a heart attack, the directors of the bank arranged for him to be buried in the bank garden!

In 1923 an Act of Parliament had provided that any human remains interred in the bank's garden court should be re-interred in Nunhead, near Peckham, and so that is where the mortal remains of the giant William Jenkins now rest.

There is an interesting footnote to this story. William Pryde stole a number of expensive diamonds in 1889. Detectives placed his Botanic Road flat under surveillance, and Pryde was observed leaving the apartment one morning and then strolling into the nearby park. A whistle was blown, and several policemen ran into the park and arrested Pryde inside the Botanic Gardens. Pryde was searched but he did not have the stolen gemstones on his person. He had obviously known that he was being watched. He is said to have dug a walking cane into an area of soft soil and put the diamonds down the hole, before covering it over with his foot.

As far as I know, those diamonds, which were valued at £20,000 in 1889, were never found.

MR SPHINX

One stormy evening at Woolton Hall in 2003, I gave an illustrated talk on the subject of the supernatural, which included several tales on the subject of vampires. After the talk, Susan, a distinguished-looking woman of eighty, approached me and told me how much she had enjoyed the stories and slide show pictures. She then related an intriguing story of her own that was as good, if not better, than any of the tales I'd been telling to people that evening. This is the account she gave.

Susan was born in Northumberland in 1923, and her mother, a teacher of English and Latin, brought Susan to Liverpool in 1933. Susan's father had deserted her mother just before the girl's birth. In the leafy lanes of suburban Aigburth, ten-year-old Susan and her mother settled into a beautiful house on Waverley Road. However, the rent for the fine residence was barely covered by the money Susan's mother brought in from her job as a private tutor.

In the autumn of 1933, a tall, smartly-dressed stranger with coal-black hair and penetrating green eyes called at the house, and told Susan's mother, in a foreign accent, that he would like to learn to speak English. The man's name, Raymond Sphinx, struck Susan as odd, to say the least. Susan's mother explained that many foreigners choose their own names to replace their real, exotic-sounding surnames, in order to blend in to the country they are living in. Mr Sphinx was quite handsome, and as Susan related this tale, she recalled how her mother seemed totally mesmerised by the debonair foreigner, who seemed to be about thirty-five years of age. He was so courteous and sophisticated, and must have been an excellent student, as he was soon speaking with a fine, mellifluous English accent.

Children are very perceptive and discerning when it comes to seeing through the pretensions of adults, and young Susan thought there was something decidedly uncanny about Mr Sphinx. He seemed to appear out of nowhere whenever he visited for his lessons, and throughout the early summer of 1934, Susan watched him walk out on to a veranda – and when she followed, he had vanished. When she mentioned this to her mother, she was accused of having an overactive imagination.

Some time later though, Susan's mother said she too had seen Raymond walk on to the veranda and then seemingly disappear into thin air. She even mentioned the incident to him on the following day, but he just smiled his enigmatic smile and said that he had slipped past her but she hadn't noticed him. Susan's mother said nothing, but knew that simply had not been the case at all.

Mr Sphinx continued to come to the house, long after he needed to, as he now spoke English as perfectly as Susan's mother. Then it slowly dawned on Susan that her mother was romantically involved with the foreigner, and on many nights she would listen to him as he sat at the piano in the drawing room, bringing forth soul-stirring concertos of Mozart and Beethoven. Some of the other, unknown melodies sounded mysterious and romantic, and they brought tears to the eyes of Susan's mother.

The multi-talented Mr Sphinx was also an accomplished storyteller, and on winter evenings would sit before a blazing fire with Susan by his side and tell her tales of kings, queens, and ordinary people of long ago. He would also describe the daring missions of King Arthur and his Knights of the Round Table, and a saga about two young lovers on opposing sides during the Wars of the Roses. Raymond told these stories with such skill, that his listeners almost believed they were actually there, in the midst of the romance and intrigue.

Susan's mother's liking for Mr Sphinx must have waned, because she became involved with another man in 1936, and Raymond decided to leave but, before he went, he produced a single blood-red rose, backed with maidenhair fern and gave it to thirteen-year-old Susan, who was heart-broken at the idea of him leaving her life. Raymond whispered the word 'Zuzana' – an old Slavic word for the rose – and said that he would return one day when she was older, and declared that his love for her was undying. He said that the rose he had given her would never die, just like the affection he felt for her. With a tear in his eye, he said, "Remember me," then left, and Susan began to sob. She begged her mother to leave her lover and to resume her relationship with Raymond, but to no avail.

The rose which Mr Sphinx had given to Susan refused to wilt, and she kept it in a special box. World War Two came and went, and still the red rose and maidenhair fern looked as fresh as the day he had given them to her.

In 1948, at the age of twenty-five, Susan married a thirty-one-year-old man named Ralph, and moved with him just around the corner from her mother, to live over the grocery shop he owned. Susan's mother was ill at this time, and her condition was exacerbated by the anger she felt towards Susan for "marrying beneath herself" as she put it, and the heartbreak she was enduring because her lover had deserted her for a much younger woman.

Weeks later, Susan's mother died from pulmonary complications, and only Susan, Ralph and a doctor were at her bedside. About a fortnight after the funeral, Susan went to the cemetery to place flowers on her mother's grave, and during the visit she had an encounter that initially shocked her. A tall man in black was already standing at the foot of her mother's grave. He turned as Susan approached. It was Raymond Sphinx, and he looked as if he hadn't aged a day since she last saw him in 1936, twelve years ago. He stood there with a faint smile on his lips; his arms outstretched to embrace Susan. He hugged and kissed her, and offered his deepest condolences. He assured her that her mother had merely shed her physical body, and that her soul had gone on to another plane of existence, where every person ends up when earthly life ceases.

Susan felt an intense physical and romantic attraction to Raymond, and she asked him to accompany her to her late mother's home on Waverley Road. At the house where Raymond had first met Susan as a child, she showed him the box containing the undying rose. Raymond embraced Susan and kissed her passionately. Not long afterwards they were making love, and throughout the act, Susan felt all her energy steadily draining away.

When the couple had finished making love, Susan felt numb and empty, and so listless, she could hardly make the effort to draw breath. A strange thought crossed her lethargic mind: had Raymond somehow siphoned off the very essence of her life force? Her lover leaned on his elbow beside her, and scanned her face, then put his palm on her forehead. Susan felt a distinct sensation of something in flux passing between his hand and her mind. Energy flowed down her spine and a strange cold tingling sensation coursed down her arms and legs.

After a while, Raymond removed his palm and then kissed Susan's cheek. She raised herself up and asked him what had just happened. She was more fascinated than afraid. She had never experienced such intense electric pleasures when her husband had made love to her. What Raymond told her shocked her to her core. Sphinx explained that he was a "type of vampire". He was nothing like the Dracula character of the Bram Stoker novel. He didn't suck blood, but he did "feed" off the life force of people – 'prana'.

Susan found herself putting on her dress without bothering to put on her underwear first. She trembled as Raymond sat at end of the bed with his head bowed and knew that he wasn't mentally unbalanced. She also knew he wasn't just trying to frighten her – he was telling the truth – she could tell by that look of sincerity in his green eyes.

"Please don't go, Susan," he said meekly.

The everlasting rose flashed into her mind. Of course! – now it all made sense. All those tales of long ago that Raymond had told around the fireside when she was a child. No wonder he had been able to make them sound so realistic – he must have been walking the earth for hundreds of years! Was he some kind of devil?

Susan didn't stop to look back as she hurried out of the bedroom in a panic, clutching her shoes. She walked barefooted down the road and only put the shoes on once she had turned the corner, from where she walked in shock back to her home above the greengrocer's. Ralph didn't even notice that her hair was in disarray, her lipstick smudged and her clothes dishevelled. Susan didn't return to her former home on Waverley Road until the next day, and when she did, she made sure that a friend went with her. She need not have worried – Raymond had gone.

In 1977, at the age of fifty-four, Susan was out shopping in Liverpool city centre when, just as she was leaving Binn's department store, she came face to face with Raymond. He still looked around thirty-five, with not a single wrinkle on his handsome face, or grey hair on his head. His green eyes sparkled as keenly as ever. He didn't recognise her at first, and he walked on past – but then he hesitated, and turned around. Not a word was spoken for a frozen moment in time. Then, as if he hadn't seen Susan for just a few days, he asked her how she was, and reached out for her hand – but she pulled away. He then suggested going to a nearby café, but she resolutely shook her head. Raymond seemed to sense that she was worried over something, and asked if her husband was well. She didn't answer. Instead, she turned and walked away, as Raymond shouted her name three times. She resolutely ignored him and walked away towards the safety of the crowds milling in and out of Woolworths.

In the Northern Hospital that evening, Susan's husband Ralph was lying in a bed, drifting in and out of a comatose state with a blood clot on his brain. The doctors had told Susan that he was in a critical condition and there was a high probability that he would not pull through. It had already been explained to her that brain surgery would be far too risky in Ralph's weakened condition.

At home, Susan fastened the top and bottom bolts of the front door, and locked her back door. Not only was she totally distraught about her husband's grave condition, but also deeply troubled about the meeting with Raymond, after all those years. She also wondered if the eerie Raymond had somehow followed her home. She took an old Bible up to the bedroom and sat up in bed, listening to the radio. She reached for the old Bible and opened it at random. She scanned a passage about the transfiguration of Christ, and for some reason it made her think about Raymond. With shame, she recalled the strange, unearthly sensations she had experienced when she was in the bed with him all those years ago, and of that mysterious word he spoke – 'prana'.

At almost three in the morning, Susan drifted into a fitful sleep that was haunted by dreams of Raymond. At eight o'clock the bell of the alarm clock sounded, and she swung her legs out of the bed like an automaton, with her eyelids still stuck together. With a sinking feeling in the pit of her stomach, she went downstairs to the hall, still in her nightdress, and telephoned the hospital. She feared the worst and dreaded to hear what they would say about her husband's condition.

She was in for a massive shock. The sister on duty said that she had some very good news. Ralph was no longer on the critical list; in fact, he was sitting up in bed, eating a hearty breakfast and laughing and joking with all the nurses. He had made a recovery that was nothing short of miraculous.

Susan was dressed and ready within half an hour of hearing this wonderful news and was soon riding in a cab to the hospital. Bursting with excitement, she rushed into the room where Ralph had lain at the gates of death for almost a month … and found the bed empty. The other bed in that room, in which a young man had been recovering from a spinal injury, was also vacant. Then she heard the sound of footsteps in the corridor to her right. It was Ralph, walking along with a nurse on either side of him, supporting him as he walked along. When he saw Susan he stopped in his tracks, and she ran to him with tears welling in her eyes. She hugged him so tightly, and he kept saying, "There, there, love," as he patted her on the back.

The nurses seemed to be just as overjoyed as they were – such miraculous recoveries happened so rarely. They showed Susan and Ralph into the two-bed ward, then left to give them some privacy. Ralph told Susan a tale that made her stomach somersault. He said that a "funny-looking man" had come into his room some time after midnight. He had walked over to Pete – the young man who was lying asleep in the other bed – and had placed his hands on the young man's chest. Ralph had been barely conscious, and the whole thing had a dream-like quality. The man – who was dressed in black – then came over to Ralph's bed and placed his palms on his chest. The intense heat from the stranger's hands penetrated right through his pyjamas, and his vest, straight into his heart. Ralph felt his entire body tingling, as if he had been plugged into the electricity mains. The man then assured Ralph that he would get better soon, then left the room in absolute silence – just like a ghost.

At six o'clock in the morning, Ralph opened his eyes, feeling like a new man. He sat up, stretched and yawned, and found a Catholic priest, a doctor and three relatives surrounding the bed of the man opposite, who was obviously dying. The priest was performing the Last Rites and Pete died soon afterwards.

"You don't believe me, do you?" Ralph said to Susan, who was staring at the single red rose, backed with a stem of maidenhead fern, lying on the bedside cabinet. But she knew exactly what had happened. Raymond – or whatever his real name was – had siphoned off the life of the young man in the other bed, and had infused that life into Ralph. Why had he done this? Susan still doesn't have any answers to this question.

Before Susan left Woolton Hall that stormy night, she told me that she was convinced that Mr Sphinx was still around. "He will probably visit you if you put him in one of your books," she told me. She then bade me goodnight, and a hackney cab took her off into the night.

SPANNER FACE

Lots of people touch the nearest piece of wood when they think they have just tempted fate. In America they say "knock wood" after untimely boasting. The touching of wood after tempting fate is a ritual lost in the mists of time, but some researchers into superstitions have noted pre-Christian rituals involving the hugging of trees that were regarded as sacred, such as oak, ash, holly, or hawthorn. And in Ireland there is an old tongue-in-cheek tradition of knocking on wood to let the little people know that you are thanking them for any good luck received.

One of the most gruesome incidents of someone tempting fate took place in Liverpool in the 1960s. Twenty-five-year-old Joan Dymond was said to have been the most beautiful woman in Liverpool at the time. The year was 1963, and Joan was living off Mill Street in south Liverpool. People who remember her claim that she could easily have ended up as a Hollywood movie star – perhaps after a few lessons in elocution. Her good looks attracted men of every age and type – but mostly the wrong type!

Despite being able to take her pick, in the summer of 1963, she married Terry, a violent former teddy boy from Huyton; an individual well known to the Liverpool and Lancashire police. Joan's parents and friends had pleaded with her to call off the wedding, but it went ahead anyway – such is the blindness of youth. The marriage couldn't have got off to a worse start, because, even during the wedding reception, Terry head-butted his own brother because of some mild insult he was supposed to have made. By the end of August, Joan had received several beatings at the hands of Terry, usually after he had returned home drunk, in the early hours of the morning.

Beaten and bruised, Joan would eventually give up and run back home to her parents, but even there she found no sanctuary, because Terry booted in their door on one occasion and threatened her father with a knife. After this incident, Joan was given shelter at the Anne Fowler Memorial Home for Women on Netherfield Road; the last refuge for many beaten wives. Terry wrote numerous pleading letters to her, saying how much he had changed, and how he had now learnt to control his violent streak. He assured her that he hadn't touched a drop of alcohol for over a fortnight and wanted nothing more than to settle down with her in a cottage in Wales. Each night he prayed for God to give him a second chance – or so he claimed in his floridly-phrased letters.

Despite a cracked rib, black eye and dislocated jaw – Joan fell for it and went back to him. He was elated at the reconciliation, and after showering her with flowers, chocolates, gifts and new clothes, he took her out in his new car. They went on the town to celebrate, and Terry was the envy of every hot-blooded male, because he once more had the beautiful goddess Joan on his arm. They jostled their way into the crowded Grapes pub on Mathew Street, where Terry barged up to the bar. A tall, quietly spoken student was sipping a glass of sarsaparilla at the bar, and when Terry rudely knocked him sideways, he protested. "Hey, mate. What d'you think you're doing?"

"Outside, come on!" Terry bawled, "No one talks to me like that."

"Very well," said the student, calmly placing his glass of sarsaparilla on the counter and making his way to the door.

Terry was taken aback by his lack of nerves. He watched him leave the pub, and was about to follow him through the door, when a friend of his warned him not to go. He told Terry that the student was a brilliant amateur middle-weight boxer who fought for his college. Terry took off his knuckleduster, and after pondering on the situation for a minute or two, bought a pint of sarsaparilla and told his friend to take it outside to the student. The student luckily saw the funny side of the gesture and came back into the pub smiling. Joan, who had been cringing in a corner, breathed a sigh of relief; it was turning into a good night with no violence for once.

During the evening, Terry even took part in a few arm-wrestling competitions, and didn't take it personally when he lost. By ten-thirty, he was sitting in a corner of the pub with a drunken Joan sitting on his knee, and they were laughing and singing. There was a sudden lull in the noisy chatter of the pub. The singing stopped, the conversationalists fell silent, and the laughter ceased. Something was moving through the pub, among the drinkers. It was something that cackled. It wore a headscarf, and it sidled over to the corner where Joan and Terry were sitting – it was Spanner Face.

Joan was almost struck sober at the horrific sight and Terry gasped with revulsion. The woman with the headscarf had a grossly disfigured face. The forehead and chin protruded like the points of a crescent moon, and the face was concave and mostly absent. Viewed side on, the face was C-shaped, like the gripping end of a spanner, hence the unfortunate woman's cruel nickname. She muttered something to Joan and Terry but neither heard her words, as they were too overwhelmed by the deformity of her face.

"Can you spare a woodbine, my dears?" she said once more, holding out her hand.

"God almighty! What happened to your face, love?" Terry asked, hoping for a cheap laugh at the poor woman's expense. He attempted a false belly laugh, but the hush around the premises was almost deafening, and his laugh died away, to be replaced with an embarrassed smile. Everyone looked away from the woman.

At last the silence was broken when Joan hid her face in Terry's jacket and giggled nervously.

"Funny isn't it?" Terry remarked, addressing the silent drinkers, "We've got the most beautiful girl in Liverpool and the ugliest old hag in Liverpool in the same pub."

"You're tempting fate, mister," said the unsightly woman under her breath.

Then the door opened and in came a youth in high spirits, singing a Beatles hit. He looked around at the subdued drinkers, and saw that most of them were staring down into their glasses, "Who's died? Is this a bleedin' wake or somethin'?"

Spanner Face turned abruptly and walked out the door, passing the hapless youth who rapidly stepped out of her way when he glimpsed the awful sight under the headscarf. There was a stir of conversation, and within less than a minute, the laughter, chatting and singing had been resumed to form the usual din in the smoky atmosphere. Terry enquired about the disfigured woman, and a few people shook their heads and explained that she was a gypsy of some sort who brought bad luck, unless you gave her what she asked for. They nervously told Terry that the woman's nickname was Spanner Face, but Terry and Joan didn't smile when they heard this.

At three o'clock that morning, Joan woke up with an agonising pain in one of her back teeth. She opened her mouth wide and peered into the bathroom mirror. She was alarmed to find that there was blood oozing from the gums around the aching tooth. She took some painkillers, but they made no difference, and the toothache was soon excruciating. Terry plied her with a concoction of milk and rum, but it too did nothing to alleviate the pain, and Joan started to cry.

She had to endure the terrible agony all over the weekend, but early on Monday morning, Terry drove her to the dentist's surgery. The dentist took a quick look at the back tooth and immediately recoiled. "I'm afraid this is serious," he said.

"What do you mean?" Joan asked, her beautiful eyes brimming with tears.

"Please, just go at once to the hospital … as soon as you can. I'm afraid it looks like gangrene," said the dentist.

Terry sped through red traffic lights to get his wife to the hospital. When Joan told a nurse about the dentist's comments, she was taken at once into a room to be examined by a surgeon. He looked as shocked as the dentist when he shone a light into Joan's mouth. Within the hour, Joan's parents had arrived at the hospital. They sat with Terry in a waiting room, chain smoking and trying to take in the graveness of the situation.

Forms were signed by Terry, giving the surgeon permission to operate on Joan, who by now was in no fit state to give her own consent, having been given morphine. The surgeon explained the urgency; gangrene from tooth decay had caused a life-threatening abscess to form. It was imperative that it be removed as soon as possible, to stop it spreading throughout Joan's bloodstream, which would kill her.

Joan was wheeled into theatre and the hours dragged by for her anxious relatives. Then, after a gruelling eight hours, the operation finally ended. The gangrenous area had been removed – but at a terrible cost. Joan's parents and Terry were told to go home and rest, as Joan would not be conscious or well enough to receive visitors for a while.

Two days later, Joan's mother and father tiptoed into the small private room to see their daughter for the first time since the operation, but all they could see was an inert figure lying on the bed, her face bandaged like an Egyptian mummy. Terry visited later in the day but couldn't elicit a single spoken response from his wife. Three days later, Joan's parents and Terry were present at her bedside as the bandages were changed, and all three recoiled when they saw what the radical surgery had done to her beautiful face. Entire chunks of it were missing, and most of the lower jaw had been hacked away. Joan's mother fainted at the disfigurement, and Terry was glad that she had collapsed, because it gave him an excuse to leave the room as he carried her out into the corridor.

What little remained of Joan's face was unrecognisable, yet chillingly familiar. Then it dawned on Terry that she now looked exactly like Spanner Face, the old woman who had approached them in the pub on the night she had been taken ill.

"Terry, please stay with her," pleaded Joan's mother when she came to. "You won't leave her, will you?"

Without answering, Terry, true to form, callously turned his back on the stricken woman and hurried straight down the long corridor and out of the hospital, already planning the divorce. When he reached the hospital gates, he saw an old flower seller, who slowly turned to face him. It was Spanner Face. She cackled horribly as he fled.

The once lovely Joan eventually recovered her health, but lived the rest of her life as a recluse at her parents' home on Windsor Street, unable to face the world with her terrible disfigurement. She is thought to have died in the early 1980s.

HOODED HARBINGER OF DEATH

One cold evening in October, 1974, nine-year-old Samantha was walking with her ten-year-old friend Joanne down a secluded path at Sherdley Park, near St Helens, when she saw a strange sight. At the end of the lane, directly beneath the thin crescent moon, stood a figure resembling a hooded monk in a long black habit. Joanne couldn't see anything. Then, without warning, a car came screeching round the bend in the lane up ahead. It swerved violently from side to side as the driver wrestled with the steering wheel to regain control over the car, but his attempt failed and the car slammed into a tree, coming to a dead halt. The noise of the impact was deafening – the shatter of glass; metalwork being twisted and flattened against the tree trunk; tyres bursting and steam escaping from the burst radiator. Instantaneously, as the car concertinered into the tree, a figure came flying headfirst through the front windscreen – just like those dummies in the road safety adverts. In a shower of glass, the figure hit the ground with a dull thump, which forced its head to turn violently and snapped its neck like a twig.

Samantha and Joanne screamed and screamed, overcome with the horror of what they had just witnessed. Meanwhile, the spectral monk, who had watched the accident from the bottom of the lane, flitted across the road towards the crash victim's mangled body, fading away when it reached him. Only Samantha had been able to see that hooded figure, and long after the trauma of the car crash had faded away, the memory of the sinister ghost remained – vivid and all too real – and often featuring in her nightmares. Her mother and father tried to soothe their daughter by telling her that the monk had been nothing more than a trick of the light, but Samantha knew better, and she was to encounter what appeared to have been some type of Grim Reaper again, on one further occasion.

In 1979, Samantha was a fourteen-year-old living with her family in the Croxteth area of Liverpool, and on the Monday evening of 5 November of that year – Guy Fawkes Night – she was looking forward to going to a friend's house on Carr Lane, for a bonfire night party. As she set off, she took a deep breath, which further fuelled her excitement; the air was filled with sulphurous fumes and the skies alive with coloured flares and rockets. A full moon loomed over Croxteth on the eastern horizon, bringing everything into sharp focus. Samantha couldn't wait to get to the display that her friend's parents would be putting on in their back garden, and so she strode down Stonebridge Lane with an enthusiastic spring in her step. All her eager anticipation instantly drained away, however, when she suddenly came upon the black monk again.

A hackney cab had just pulled up outside a terraced house, and two women, aged about seventy something, alighted from the vehicle and walked up the path towards the house. They were completely oblivious to the eerie black figure who suddenly sped towards them out of nowhere. Samantha froze in her tracks as she watched the supernatural entity that was just thirty yards away. From this distance she could see that, instead of a living person, there was a skull beneath the hood, and its hands and feet were also skeletal. Not only was the monk's appearance alarming, but the behaviour of this spine-chilling figure – which again, could apparently only be seen by Samantha – was also decidedly odd and unnerving.

The mad monk danced around the two pensioners as they walked along, then dashed ahead of them and started to stamp its bony foot on their front door step. The figure then vanished, as one of the two women opened the door with a key. By this time, they had both noticed Samantha, who was staring at them open-mouthed near their front gate. The women stood in the hallway, watching the teenaged girl, suspecting that she was up to no good. Samantha pulled herself together and hurried off down the dark lane to her friend's house. She started to tell her friend and her friend's parents what she had seen, but they obviously didn't believe her, so she gave up.

A few days later, Samantha was walking up the same road where she had seen the dancing skeleton on bonfire night – when she saw something that made her stomach churn. A woman was carrying funeral wreaths from a car into the house where the two elderly ladies lived. Had one of them died? And was the monk-like figure some kind of angel of death?

Samantha was telling her friend in Carr Lane what she had just seen, when the girl's parents overheard her. They told Samantha that not just one, but both old women who had lived in the house in question had died within minutes of one another in mysterious circumstances. They had been sisters, and apparently, one of them had died from hypothermia, and the other had then suffered a stroke – probably when she came across her sister lying dead on the floor of the hallway. It was a terrible double tragedy which had shocked and saddened the whole neighbourhood. To this day, Samantha still lives in fear of another meeting with the weird harbinger of death.

A DANCE WITH DEATH

In the summer of 1885, a small slender woman with a pale childish face visited Liverpool. She was twenty-nine-year-old Elizabeth Berry of Oldham, and she had come to visit a relative who lived on Duke Street. After the visit, Elizabeth journeyed across the Mersey on the ferry to see a cousin over at New Brighton, and ended up staying at the resort for three days. On the last day, Elizabeth entered the tent of the expensive and controversial fortune-teller, Madame Rosamund, who had intrigued her since the day she arrived. Rosamund, who claimed to be of Romany descent, broke the golden rule of fortune telling: never reveal the details of a forthcoming death to a client. "You have had many deaths in your life, Elizabeth," said Rosamund in a low voice, as she peered knowingly into the dark glassy depths of a purple-tinted crystal ball.

"Yes, yes, I have," Elizabeth replied, then queried: "But how do you know my name?"

"Your husband ... gone, your son ... gone" she whispered.

A shiver of apprehension shot down Elizabeth's spine. What the fortune-teller said was true. Four years ago, Elizabeth's invalid husband, Thomas, had died suddenly, and just over a year later, their son had also died. At the time of his death he had been sleeping in a damp bed in Blackpool. Elizabeth had received the sum of seventy pounds from an insurance policy when her husband died, and five pounds for her son's death.

"Oh! The shadow is reaching out now for your daughter ..." said Rosamund, eyeing her terrified client from under her jet black lashes.

Rosamund's large dark eyes widened and probed deeper into the very nucleus of the crystal sphere. Elizabeth already felt faint, but there was another terrible revelation still to come. Oblivious to Elizabeth's evident distress, Rosamund continued to reel off what lay in store for the young widow in the future.

"You will dance with a tall dark stranger, and he will drop you and take your life. His eyes are brown – they twinkle like the stars – and he will captivate you, but he will surely kill you. His eyes will be full of tears when he sees what he has done. You will then go to the terrible place of darkness and gnashing of teeth."

Trembling, Elizabeth stood up, and backed away from the sinister seer. The unrepentant Madame Rosamund covered the crystal ball with a dark green velvet cloth and gently shook her head, "I only read the future, my dear, warts and all."

Some time later, Elizabeth was invited to a ball in Oldham by her local butcher, thirty-five-year-old Tom Whittaker. Elizabeth politely declined the invitation, concerned lest he should turn out to be the tall dark man with the twinkling brown eyes who would kill her. He was certainly tall and dark-eyed, and Elizabeth had often winced at the way the young butcher would hack the blood-drained carcasses with his enormous meat cleaver. She shuddered at the recollection. No! She would rather stay at home with her knitting, thank you very much!

A month after that, old Mr Hargreaves, the counter clerk from the local post office, invited the pretty young widow to a soirée at the local church hall. Mr Hargreaves was bald and blue-eyed, so there was no way he could be the brown-eyed killer foretold by the fortune-teller, and she accepted his invitation, thinking it would make a pleasant, if rather unexciting, change.

So Elizabeth Berry walked hand in hand with a man old enough to be her father into a church hall one hot July night in 1885. The two of them joined in the dancing, until, at one point in the evening, Mr Hargreaves sat down to rest his weary legs, leaving Elizabeth on the periphery of the dance floor, still eager to join in the dancing. She made a very pretty picture, with her black curly hair tied up with a silk crimson bow, and her ivory white dress prettily adorned with pearls and pink roses. Her round face was childish, and being powdered and flushed from all the dancing, she didn't look a day over sixteen. She did not have to wait long before a tall man with hair as black and curly as Elizabeth's own approached her. He invited her to dance, but she shook her head and cast her eyes down, nervously.

Death had arrived.

"Oh, come now, don't be such a wallflower," teased the man in a deep voice, betraying an American accent.

Without waiting for a reply, the tall dark stranger grabbed her hand and Elizabeth felt dizzy and faint. She almost fell towards him. Her heart was palpitating. She was a helpless doll in his muscular arms, as he waltzed her wildly across the dance floor. Everything swirled: the chandelier swam overhead, and the other couples spun past like mad dervishes. The American's cologne was as masculine and overpowering as himself. The heady aroma stifled Elizabeth Berry, yet she had never felt more alive in all of her twenty-nine years.

When the musicians stopped playing and the waltz ended, Elizabeth and the American were out of breath, and both were obviously filled with lust for one another. Growing increasingly agitated, Mr Hargreaves had been watching all these goings on from the sidelines and at the earliest opportunity he grabbed Elizabeth's arm, upon which the American, a Texan whose name was Brett, said, "Sir, may I compliment you? Your daughter is truly the finest English Rose I have set eyes upon since coming to this country."

Hargreaves ample cheeks puffed with fury, and in no uncertain terms, he told Brett that he was not Elizabeth's father, but a good friend. Two other men who had been eyeing Elizabeth Berry with desire, seized their opportunity and confronted the American, accusing him of insulting a senior citizen of Oldham. A serious fight ensued, and Hargreaves and another man bundled Elizabeth out of the hall and took her home. At her gate, Hargreaves made a pass at Elizabeth, but she laughingly told him that she was not interested in him in a physical way, merely as a friend. When Hargreaves heard the bare, unpalatable truth, he surprised her by bursting into tears, then sucking his thumb!

That night, Elizabeth lay awake in her bed, thinking constantly of Brett's wide manly shoulders, his sleek black hair, and those dark penetrating brown eyes. She was so totally smitten that she convinced herself that Madame Rosamund had lied to her – the handsome American couldn't possibly do her any harm.

The summer mellowed as the weeks passed, and in the late August of 1885, a young local policeman named Bob Oakley invited Elizabeth to another ball, this time in Manchester. The ball had been organised by the Manchester Police Force, and most of the people attending the occasion were either policemen, ex-policemen, or their relatives. Young Oakley never danced once with Elizabeth Berry, as he didn't get a chance. She had created quite a stir, and the hot-blooded police constables crowded about her and queued up to take her in their arms and sweep her across the dance floor.

Of all the men who waylaid her that evening, only one caught the eye and heart of Elizabeth, and his name was James. He was tall, with hair as black as coal, and eyes of smouldering lignite brown. They flashed with emotion as James twirled her effortlessly around the dance floor. Elizabeth sat at a table with James and found him to be the most perfect, courteous, gallant and handsome man she had ever set eyes upon. She told him about her bereavements, and how she hoped to rebuild a life for herself and her daughter and become a nurse at the Oldham Workhouse, but when Elizabeth tried to discover if James was a policeman, he steered the conversation away in another direction. All Elizabeth was able to ascertain from the conversation was that James was a bachelor. Anyway, whatever his occupation, she argued to herself, he was obviously a kind and caring man. Yet again, although James matched perfectly Rosamund's description of Elizabeth's future killer, her emotions were powerful enough to blot out the fortune teller's awful predictions.

Then came a most curious coincidence. James learned that Elizabeth's surname was the same as his – Berry. If they married, James mused, Elizabeth would still retain her original surname. All this talk of marriage gave Elizabeth the courage to hint that perhaps they should keep in touch, but James Berry sighed and told her that his work would be taking him to another town, far away, in the morning. After that, he was needed in another part of the country, and such was the itinerant nature of his job, that he was rarely in one place for more than a day at a time.

That night, James guided Elizabeth out on to a balcony, as every other couple savoured the last waltz. They clung to each other and kissed passionately by the light of the full moon, as the last strains of the music filled their ears. James said he knew in his soul that he would meet Elizabeth again one day, and when that day came, he would give up his work and marry her. They both cried on the balcony beneath the moon and stars. But, within half an hour, James was travelling east, and Elizabeth was travelling west back to Oldham.

Elizabeth Berry worked for a while as a nurse at the Oldham Workhouse, but she did not really enjoy the work, and inwardly believed that she deserved a better station in life. Her annual salary was just twenty-five pounds, and that was not nearly enough to pay for good clothes and a decent lifestyle. She had a strange dual personality; kindness itself to the patients one day, and cruel and heartless the next. There were also strange rumours circulating about the daughter Elizabeth Berry hardly mentioned. This was eleven-year-old Edith Annie Berry, whom she had placed in the care of an aunt.

In January 1887, Elizabeth invited the child back into her life, but unfortunately, the girl fell gravely ill within days of the reunion. Elizabeth Berry's neighbours, who had no doubt already decided that she was a bit of a flighty piece, because of all her admirers, whispered that the widow was cursed, but others attributed Edith Annie's illness to a rather more sinister cause. After all, it was widely known that Edith's mother had recently taken out an insurance policy on her daughter, and stood to receive ten pounds compensation if the girl should die. This was true – however, Elizabeth Berry had also taken out a second policy that would pay out one hundred pounds to either Edith or her mother, depending on who lived the longer.

Little Edith Annie died in agony at five o'clock in the morning on the day after she had fallen ill. Given that Elizabeth Berry had now lost a husband, a son and a daughter to mysterious illnesses, and had received insurance payouts in each case, foul play was suspected. A Dr Patterson and several other doctors performed a post-mortem on Edith Annie – and discovered a powerful poison – possibly sulphuric acid – both in her stomach and in samples of her vomit.

Several people who had known Elizabeth came forward and expressed their belief that she had even murdered her own mother with poison, as she had died in similar circumstances. So Elizabeth's mother was duly exhumed – and poison was indeed found in her stomach. Other former friends added to the case for the prosecution, claiming that Elizabeth not only smoked opium, but was an immoral flirt who read sensational lurid novels. All Elizabeth Berry could say in her defence was that if, as the prosecution claimed, she had poisoned her mother, husband and children, then she must have been insane at the time.

However, her pleas of insanity went unheeded and she was tried, found guilty and sentenced to death for the murder of her mother by poisoning. A second case – that she had murdered Edith Annie – was not brought before the courts. The date set for her execution was Monday, 14 March 1887, and the place was Kirkdale Prison. That fateful day soon arrived, and hundreds of Liverpudlians who had eagerly read the lurid accounts of the dreadful poisonings, braved the snow and icy winds as they gathered at the foot of the prison walls. Immediately prior to the execution, the hangman visited Elizabeth in her cell. She looked up as he entered and realised at once that it was James Berry, the man she had danced with two years before. When they saw one another, they stood motionless, both of them in shock. The prison warders glanced back and forth between Elizabeth and James, until one of them said, "Have you met before?"

James Berry nodded, and asked if he could spend a few private moments alone with the condemned woman.

"Of course," said the senior warder. "Knock when you want us to collect her."

The hangman and the murderess embraced in the cold dark quietly. Madame Rosamund's prophecy had come to pass … You will dance with a tall dark stranger, and he will drop you and take your life. His eyes are brown, they twinkle like the stars, and he will captivate you, but he will surely kill you. His eyes will be full of tears when he sees what he has done …

James assured Elizabeth that her death would be quick and painless. He would make sure of that in the positioning of the knot around her beautiful, delicate neck. Outside in the prison yard, warders were sprinkling sand over the snowy path to the gallows, to make sure that Elizabeth would not slip. Meanwhile, in the cell, the hangman was saying, "I never forgot you in those two years, Elizabeth. No woman has eyes as beautiful as yours. No woman on this earth has touched my heart the way that you did that moonlit summer night."

The hands of the prison clock ticked relentlessly on, and soon the warders grew impatient. They knocked on the cell door and asked James Berry if he was ready. In a choked voice, he replied that he was. The chaplain accompanied Elizabeth and the warders and the executioner to the gallows. James

Berry climbed up first and readied himself for the dreadful task that lay ahead. He glanced down and saw that Elizabeth had fainted. Two warders carried her up to the scaffold, and she was positioned over the trapdoor – or 'the drop', as it was known.

As James Berry pinioned her feet together and adjusted the straps, Elizabeth regained consciousness, and gasped as the heavy noose was adjusted around her neck. "May the Lord have mercy upon me," she whispered. "Lord receive my spirit."

The white hood was gently placed over her head, and she kissed the hangman's hand as he pulled the cloth over her soft face. The chaplain prayed in a low muttering voice, and James Berry closed his eyes as he threw the lever which drew the bolt. In an instant, the trapdoor sprang open and Elizabeth Berry plunged into eternity.

James Berry would later voluntarily retire from his grisly occupation and openly condemned capital punishment as an obscene abomination. People often asked him why he had abandoned and attacked his own profession in such a way, and Berry would always refuse to give a satisfactory explanation, but I'm sure that Elizabeth's death was the sole reason.

WITHOUT YOU

In the Garston area of Liverpool, in September 1974, twenty-two-year-old Beth moved into a two-bedroom house with her two-year-old daughter. Her partner Jeff had recently deserted her, and Beth's friends, most of whom she had known since her schooldays, often visited her and encouraged her to go out.

The house was small but cosy and Beth had been looking forward to living in it. However, from the very first day that she moved in, she immediately sensed the faint presence of a previous female resident. Beth was not in the least bit psychic, but she couldn't shake off the feeling. Perhaps it was the aroma of Mansion House furniture polish in the hall, or the strong scent of lavender which greeted her nose in the living room. Beth had no washing machine or tumble dryer when she moved in, and she hadn't really been prepared for living on her own. She looked at the pile of baby's washing and sighed, then some strange instinct guided her to a cupboard in the kitchen, where she found a large tin box crammed with clothing pegs, wire wool, a length of clothes line, candles, dusters and other knick-knacks. Next to the box there were several old but half-full and still usable boxes of Omo washing powder, a can of Brasso metal polish, and a tube of Ajax bleach powder. Beth didn't yet possess a television set either, so she was very grateful for the small transistor radio she found in another of the kitchen cupboards. It looked pretty old, yet it worked perfectly well. Beth tuned into Radio One, her favourite station, listened to a few songs, then switched it off.

Beth's friends brought round food and drink for the house-warming party that she held one Sunday evening, which went on until three in the morning. By two o'clock in the morning, all the girls who had come to the party with their boyfriends had left, but Ruth and Andrea, two of Beth's closest friends, stayed on long after the last guests had gone, helping her to clean up the mess. They then sat around the old open fire, smoking and gossiping. Beth went to put the kettle on the gas stove during their conversation, and as she was filling the kettle, she caught a fleeting glimpse of a woman's face staring back at her through the kitchen window. She shrieked, dropped the kettle into the sink, then ran back into the living room to Ruth and Andrea.

"What's happened? What's the matter ... you look like you've seen a ghost," Andrea said. She imagined that Beth had perhaps seen a spider or a mouse, she knew she hated both.

"There's ... there's someone in the back garden ... some woman," Beth replied.

Ruth went to the window and peeped through the gap in the curtains. Armed with the poker which she had picked up from the grate, Andrea also went into the kitchen. She switched off the light and peered through the glass panes. She couldn't see anything unusual, just the starry sky and the barely discernible silhouettes of treetops and the chimneys of the house that backed on to the small garden. "What was she like?" she asked.

"It was all so fast," said Beth. "She looked really pale, and her eyes were very black, as if she'd been crying. There were streaks running down from them where her mascara had run."

"Wonder what she was doing in your back garden?" Andrea said. "Have you seen her before? Maybe she's a neighbour who's had too much to drink and went into the wrong back garden."

At that moment, the old transistor radio suddenly switched itself on, causing the three women to jump. Earlier, on Sunday evening, Radio 1 had played the Top 30 songs between 5pm and 7pm, then the station had joined Radio 2. No soft-voiced Radio 2 DJ was heard on the radio this time however, just the unnerving sobs of a woman. Moments later, the Harry Nilsson song, *Without You* – which had been at number one a few years before – blared out of the radio at full volume.

Beth picked the radio up and tried to switch it off – but even though she thumbed the volume wheel down until it clicked, the melancholic song continued to play with such intensity, that the radio's speakers vibrated. Ruth took the radio from Beth and located a small removable panel which covered the battery compartment. She removed the panel with the intention of removing the batteries – only to find that there were no batteries in the radio.

As Ruth and Beth looked at one another in puzzlement, the song emanating from the baffling radio finally faded away. There were no further supernatural incidents that night and when dawn came, Ruth and Andrea left. Beth quickly got into bed and buried herself beneath the blankets, unable to get the pale face of the crying woman out of her head. The sobs she had heard on the radio also replayed incessantly in the young woman's mind.

Three days later, Andrea and Ruth both visited Beth's home again at 7pm. Once more they heard the sounds of the same song they'd heard before when the radio had played without a power source. This time the song was not as loud, but still audible enough to be easily recognisable. Beth shuddered, because earlier in the day she had thrown that infernal radio into the dustbin outside. Following the sound of the song, Andrea and Ruth peeped through the doorway into the kitchen, and there was the transistor radio on the draining board adjacent to the sink. All three women entered the kitchen, and Andrea was the first to dare to pick up the radio. Beth opened the door to the back garden and held her hands out for the radio. "Give me that thing. It's going back in the bin," she said.

The presence of Ruth and Andrea gave her enough confidence to go out into dark garden to dump the radio back in the dustbin. She had no idea how the accursed thing had managed to find its way back into the house, and it was not something she wanted to dwell on. She shoved the radio deep into the refuse, and slammed the lid down with a clang. Whatever is going on, it isn't going to make me live in fear, thought Beth. Turning back towards the house, she was stopped short by the sight of her two friends standing motionless in the kitchen doorway. Their heads were tilted slightly upwards and their faces were looking at something with expressions of shock and horror. Beth nervously turned and followed the line of their gaze until she found herself looking at a tree at the bottom of the garden. There was something unfamiliar dangling from the black tree branches silhouetted against the ultramarine blue sky of evening; a long black shape that slowly rotated until it presented a pale face. The likeness was unmistakable – it was the very same face that had ever so briefly peeped in at Beth through the kitchen window. Its eyes were large black circles with mascara streaking from them.

Beth screamed and threw her hands up to her face to blot out the image of the hanged woman spiralling gently anti-clockwise, suspended from the second branch of the tree next to the shed, about twelve feet above the ground.

The three women rushed out of the house via the front door and called to two men who were passing by. They told them about the woman hanging in the garden, and the men, seeing how upset they were, followed them into the house and hurried down the hallway. Andrea led them through the kitchen to the back door that was still ajar. The men stepped into the garden and asked where the hanged woman was. Andrea pointed to the tree – and saw that the figure had now vanished. The men scanned the garden, then glanced back at the three women with lightly veiled scepticism. They felt that they had been the subject of some kind of practical joke and soon left, walking quickly down the hallway and back out into the street, ignoring Andrea's assurances that there really had been a woman hanging in the garden.

Understandably, Beth soon decided to move from that

Garston house, and many years later, she heard a disturbing story about the place that explained the apparition. Apparently, a twenty-three-year-old woman named Nancy had hanged herself in the garden after her boyfriend had dumped her. At the time of the split, the popular but sad song *Without You* had reached number one in the pop charts, and was constantly played on the radio. The song must have summed up all of the heartbreak which Nancy was experiencing at the time, because the neighbours complained that the inconsolable young woman would turn the radio up to full volume whenever *Without You* was played on air.

Nancy became increasingly depressed and desperate and eventually obtained a length of sturdy rope. It is said that she borrowed it from a neighbour, using the excuse that she needed it to tow a car. The broken-hearted Nancy then climbed up on to the roof of the garden shed and from there to the branch of the tree from which she hanged herself.

Perhaps Nancy is still not at rest, as there have been numerous reports of the frightening, swollen-eyed apparition of her hanging at the house in Garston over the years.

THE CUPID'S BOW MURDER

Up in the northern extremities of Northumberland, at a place called Wooler, on the Scottish border, is a series of ancient markings engraved on sandstone boulders over three thousand years ago. Their meaning continues to baffle archaeologists. The markings are unique in the British Isles, and they include a group of concave spherical shapes, each around ten inches in diameter, whilst another is the carving of an adult footprint. Among the mysterious carvings there is an arrow and a heart, hewn out of the stone, and this strikes me as a rather black coincidence, because nearby, in the 1870s, the mystifying Cupid's Bow murder took place, and the man suspected of carrying out the ultimate crime of passion came from Liverpool.

In 1875, fifty-year-old widower James Thorpe of Little Bongs, Knotty Ash, inherited a vast fortune, left to him by his spinster aunt. Rather than investing his newfound wealth, he chose instead to travel the world.

In Sicily, in 1876, he met a young woman who was to change the course of his life. Her name was Rosalia Salvatore, a small, shapely attractive eighteen-year-old. Thorpe fell instantly in love with the brown-eyed beauty and, in a rather shameful transaction, bought her from her father. The girl was brought to England, and Thorpe was soon showing her off at every soirée and dance. However, Rosalia was so beautiful, that when she graced the dance floor, the men only noticed her and not her middle-aged, nondescript partner – it was as if Thorpe had become invisible in her presence, such was his fiancée's stunning Latin beauty. All the women, on the other hand, instantly hated the poor girl because their husbands and fiancés were mesmerised by her good looks.

A steady stream of vitriolic green-inked hate letters were sent from anonymous women to Thorpe's mansion, criticising both his and his young 'foreign' fiancée's behaviour. Thorpe endured the hate mail for months before deciding to purchase a cottage in Northumberland, near Doddington Moor, where he and Rosalia could take refuge from the green-eyed women of Liverpool's high society. At Rothbury Cottage, James and Rosalia enjoyed the secluded rural life. They walked hand in hand over the rugged heather moorland, enjoyed the birdsong which filled the coniferous forests, and pondered their love amid the prehistoric crags and ancient megalithic standing stones which dotted the area.

However, in the summer of 1877, the eternal love triangle reared its ugly head when Jem Garnock, a huge giant of a man, visited Rothbury Cottage. James Thorpe's twenty-five-year-old cousin called out of the blue, asking for employment. He'd recently fallen on hard times after losing his job as a printer's overseer because of an altercation. Broad-shouldered Jem stood at six feet and three inches high in his stocking feet, and with his long flowing black hair and walrus moustache, he was of striking appearance. The moment he set eyes on the delightful Rosalia, he fell for her, and his physical ruggedness and youth likewise instantly captivated her.

James Thorpe was no blind fool, and he quickly noticed the way his wife-to-be was eyeing his cousin, so he told Jem to return to Liverpool at once, and accused him of being a freeloading loafer. In broken English, Rosalia interposed and begged her husband to at least feed Jem before sending him on his way. Jem enjoyed a hearty meal thanks to her, but before he had time to digest it, he was shown the door. However, it seems that Jem did not return to Liverpool that night. Instead he obtained work with a team of woodcutters in the forests of the Cheviot Hills. Jem visited Rosalia in secret several times, and James soon became very suspicious when the girl asked to be alone when she embarked on her early evening strolls.

On the morning of Midsummer's Day, a ghostly mist rolled in from the North Sea and swirled over Doddington Moor and Rothbury Cottage. James Thorpe awoke to find Rosalia Salvatore absent from his bed. He looked out the window into the thick mist, and saw a spectral figure hurrying away in the distance.

Around seven o'clock that morning, Jem Garnock gently embraced Rosalia beneath the sprawling branches of a large lime tree. He started to kiss her passionately, and as he did so, he pushed her against the tree trunk. The beauty from Persephone's island gazed into Jem's slate-grey eyes and sighed, "I love you … ti amato …"

Her words of love were instantly cut short in the most brutal fashion. Something slammed hard and deep with a thud into Jem's back. The impact crushed his body against Rosalia, and she yelped in pain. Reflexively, he tried to pull away – but found himself pinned to her somehow. His back and chest felt numb. Rosalia's mouth opened wide, and blood began to trickle from the side of her lip. She gazed up at him with her stunningly beautiful eyes, but the twinkle had gone from them. They rolled upwards as the lids closed. Her head slumped forward, and came to rest on Jem's chest.

He gently lifted her head and looked down. He saw blood on his waistcoat, and a bright red bloodstain blossoming on the front of Rosalia's blouse. He felt the warm blood from both their wounds trickle down through his clothes. Something had impaled him and his forbidden love to the trunk of the lime tree. Jem cried out in agony as he desperately tried to feel what the thing was that had gone right through his chest and then through Rosalia's heart.

He managed to pull the dead girl from the tree, and felt her back. The sharp tip of an arrow protruded from it. Carrying his beloved's body, he staggered a few feet, then fell. Their bodies remained skewered together by the arrow. The mists around him seemed to darken and soon afterwards, Jem Garnock lost consciousness. He awoke some time later to find himself in a cottage, with a policeman and a doctor at his side. The doctor told him that the arrow had narrowly missed his heart, but had grazed one of his lungs. It had been a chance in a million. Unfortunately, the arrow had passed straight through him and had continued through the lady's heart.

A detective was soon at the cottage. In the course of his speculations he wondered if a stray arrow shot by someone out hunting game had been the cause of the tragedy, but Jem was quick to refute this supposition and accuse his cousin, James Thorpe. An indignant James, when questioned, told the detective that he had slept until almost eight o'clock that morning, and was suffering from heart trouble because of the shock of losing his fiancée in such a shocking way. He added that if his cousin hadn't been recovering from the arrow wound, he would have horse whipped him for courting Rosalia behind his back. The detective then asked Thorpe if he had ever used a bow and arrow, and the Liverpool businessman screamed back a vehement denial. Thorpe said that he agreed with the detective's initial theory, believing that a hunter had accidentally killed his fiancée and was probably too terrified to come forward.

Rosalia was buried in a local churchyard, and James Thorpe eventually returned to Liverpool, where several people, on hearing the circumstances of his fiancée's death, recalled that he had taken part in several archery competitions at Sefton Park five years previously. Meanwhile, Thorpe had confided to his closest friends that he was convinced that the Camorra, the secret criminal organisation in Rosalia's country, had been behind the killing and wounding. However, a man who had travelled extensively around Sicily and Italy said that the Camorra would never have killed a woman; it was taboo to do so, and completely unthinkable. Having heard this, Thorpe then suggested that perhaps they had really intended to kill his cousin and had accidentally killed Rosalia in the process.

"Then why not simply use a dagger?" asked Thorpe's friend. "That's how the Camorra usually kill. They believe in facing the victim as they kill, it's all part of their code."

James Thorpe had no answer for this and realised that he was fooling no one, and therefore decided to hide himself away. Rumours and theories about his guilt abounded, but it seems that for the remainder of his life, he was repeatedly haunted by the ghost of Rosalia in a most sinister and terrifying way.

The first supernatural incident in these series of hauntings was witnessed by Thorpe, his butler, and a maidservant at his home near Stanley Park on 21 June 1878 – the first anniversary of Rosalia's untimely death. The mantelpiece clock in the drawing room on the first floor was striking nine in the evening, and Thorpe was relaxing in his soft, leather-padded Wolsey chair, when he heard a faint crashing sound coming from somewhere in the house. It sounded like the cook dropping some dinner plates, but then he heard the screams of the young maidservant in the back parlour. Thorpe rushed out of the drawing room and looked down the stairs towards the hall, where he saw the elderly butler emerging from the back parlour, trembling and confused. "What's the matter?" Thorpe shouted down to the servant, as he hurried down the stairs.

By way of reply, the old butler made an incoherent gibbering sound, and pushed the parlour door open. What James Thorpe saw in that room turned him to ice. An arrow had been shot into his large oil portrait hanging on the wall. Shards of glass from the shattered windowpane were scattered all over the floor, where the arrow had smashed its way into the room. The maid suddenly emerged from a dark corner of the parlour and peeped over the chiffonier at Thorpe. She tried to speak but was as unintelligible as the butler. After a stiff drink, the pair of servants eventually managed to relate a very eerie account of their experiences.

Apparently, they had seen what looked like a woman in a

long white gown floating past the window. In her hand she held a longbow and an arrow, which she aimed very deliberately at the windows. She fired the arrow straight through the window, then floated off into the evening sky. James Thorpe shuddered, particularly when he realised that his fiancée had died exactly one year before. He suspected Jem Garnock of staging the 'ghost hoax' but when he made enquiries about him, he was reliably informed that he had emigrated to America.

Further incidents followed, terrorising the entire household. In the end the ghostly activities became so intense that the butler and five other servants decided to pack up and leave the house. It is said that a policeman also witnessed the ghostly female archer in the shroud, floating over the walls surrounding Thorpe's mansion in the moonlight.

James Thorpe was forced to move yet again and went to live in Ireland, and people said that he was even persecuted there by the ghost of a shroud-clad woman. Thorpe became a convert to Roman Catholicism soon afterwards and died in London in 1900, aged seventy-five.

THE PYROMANIAC

The following strange tale was investigated by a reporter from the *London Daily Chronicle* in Victorian times. It concerned an eerie self-made man who worshipped a god of fire and practised Occultism.

On the balmy Tuesday evening of 9 August 1898, a fire of mysterious origin engulfed a boarding house in St Paul's Square, off Bixteth Street in Liverpool. Four foreign sailors perished in the blaze, and as their harrowing screams echoed about the square that night, a tall, top-hatted gentleman in a cape stood nearby, accompanied by a gaggle of ragged clothed street urchins. The caped man and his little helpers stayed in a corner of the square as the local people rushed frantically back and forth with pails of water, in an effort to extinguish the blaze. The screams died away quite suddenly and then red tongues of fire spread uniformly out of the heat busted window frames and seared the guttering.

In the midst of all this turmoil, a policeman recognised the elderly gentleman lurking in the dark corner. Although he had served many years in the Liverpool Constabulary, and had witnessed many frightening and distressing sights, he experienced a shudder of revulsion when he spotted Henry Juvenal, because he had seen the same distinguished but sinister gentleman on two previous occasions – on both of which he had been watching a blaze. He watched in disgust as Juvenal smiled with satisfaction and closed his eyes, as he tilted back his head slightly, savouring the inhalation of smoke.

At that moment, the clanging bell of the horse-drawn fire engine suddenly distracted the constable as it careered into the square. Half an hour later, the well-to-do but decidedly weird pyromaniac and his gaggle of grubby barefoot children had gone.

Just over a fortnight later, Henry Juvenal was spotted once again standing amid a street gang of impoverished children in the vicinity of a large fire. On this occasion, a zoo was ablaze. Cross's Menagerie in the city was going up in smoke and the wild animals were squealing and howling as the flames roasted them alive. This time, Juvenal and his entourage of sooty-faced juveniles were moved on by the police and members of the fire brigade. One fireman, tired of seeing Henry Juvenal at the scene of every fire he attended, voiced out loud what everyone was thinking; that it was suspicious how Juvenal was always to be found in close proximity to a major fire.

Enraged that he was to be denied his perverse pleasure on this occasion, the arrogant Juvenal swung his walking cane in rage at one of the fireman, narrowly missing his helmet. A policeman, assisted by a member of the public, pushed him away from the fireman and his colleagues, but the gang of children swarmed around those apprehending the eccentric old man and clung on to their clothes. The policeman blew his shrill whistle and the children finally scattered. Juvenal backed away and swore he would take legal action against the fireman for defamation of character.

The bizarre tales concerning Henry Juvenal travelled far and wide and soon reached the ears of Alfred Robinson, a reporter for the *London Daily Chronicle*. Robinson journeyed to Liverpool and set about gathering information about the mysterious Juvenal. He discovered that he had been present when Crosby Lighthouse had been destroyed by a mystifying fire on 2 February of that year. The fire had claimed three people's lives, including the lighthouse keeper and his wife. In the course of his investigations, the reporter visited the inhabitants of St Paul's Square, where the four seamen had died in the lodging house blaze. A few of the square's residents recalled having seen the top-hatted man stroll suspiciously round the square after dark, chatting to the street children, and giving some of them money.

It was time for Robinson to call upon the enigmatic Henry Juvenal in person, and coincidentally, the day the reporter decided to go in search of the fire-obsessed old man happened to be Guy Fawkes night. There seemed to be no record of Juvenal's address in any directory, but it was generally known that his home was a distinctive red brick house on the eastern extremities of Edge Lane, between

Broadgreen and Bowring Park. Robinson finally located the grand dwelling of Henry Juvenal as night was falling. A ground mist oozed through the high, wrought iron rails of the front gates. At the top of each gatepost was the horned head of a gargoyle, and carved into the stonework of these posts, in bas-relief, were various figures of myth associated with fire, including the phoenix arising from the flames, and the fire-resistant salamander.

The gates were not locked, so Alfred Robinson was able to enter the elegant grounds of the grandiose house unhindered and he walked with some apprehension up the long curved path towards the front door. A huge black dog trotted out of the gloom and growled menacingly at the reporter, exposing its sharp, yellow fangs. The coal-black Newfoundland Labrador stopped less than six feet away from him and seemed ready to pounce, when Robinson suddenly became aware of an orange and yellow luminescence flaring up from the depths of the ground fog.

A shrill whistle was heard, and the dog's ears immediately pricked up. It then turned and loped back into the dark grey limbo of the evening vapours. Then came a row of fiery lights – a weird, torch-lit procession of some sort. The torches were heading his way, and all Robinson's instincts told him to flee, but he was a professional reporter, and decided to stand his ground; knowing from experience that it was the only way to get the facts of a story. Cowering in the bushes, or running away would not do for the *Chronicle*. Robinson feared his editor more than the strange situation at hand.

Then Henry Juvenal himself approached, carrying a sputtering flaming torch aloft and wearing a pointed hat and flowing robes like the Grand Wizard of the Ku Klux Klan. Surrounding him were five boys, also wearing pointed hats, and each carrying lit torches like their adult leader.

"Sir, you are trespassing!" bawled Juvenal, "What is your business here?"

"Are you Henry Juvenal?" asked Robinson, catching a quick glimpse of the black dog's eyes, ominously reflecting the torchlight.

"I am, and what is it to you?" asked Juvenal imperiously, as he squinted at the reporter.

"Sir, you are a most difficult man to contact. I have come from the *Daily Chronicle* in London to write an article about you," said Robinson, expecting to be attacked at any minute.

Instead, the deeply etched features of Juvenal's face softened, and he seemed bemused and even flattered. The reporter was invited to the bonfire party which Juvenal and the children had set up on the land at the back of the house. Robinson assumed that the bonfire party was to be a normal Guy Fawkes one, but when he turned the corner, he saw something very sinister; towering above him was a stone idol, and something was kicking and wriggling in its arms. Trying to remain calm, Robinson talked rather incoherently about the rumours and allegations of arson surrounding Juvenal, as he followed the old man and his little disciples towards the idol.

"Sir, may I ask you what this is?" he enquired, and produced a small notebook and pencil with which he set about describing the statue in shorthand. The deity was about eighteen feet in height, and looked as if it was made of basalt. It had the head of a horned bull, and the fearsome face of a devil with a mouth full of large fangs. Two arms that stretched out from the statue held a live sheep. The animal was bound to the stone claws of the idol, and seemed almost snug as it nestled against several holes in the statue's chest. These holes led down into a hollowed-out section at the base of the strange idol which was crammed with kindling and firewood.

"This is my idol of Moloch, an underrated god of the

ancients. They burned babies on replicas of this statue long ago," said Juvenal matter-of-factly, "but the damned authorities make it hard to do that today."

Alfred Robinson's blood ran cold. He did his best to try and talk Juvenal and the children out of the cruel live cremation of the sheep, but the children seemed transfixed by their leader, and when he uttered several unintelligible commands, the minors ceremonially hurled their torches at the firewood in Moloch's hollow stomach. Within minutes, a searing hungry fire erupted from the idol's chest like the flames of a blowtorch. The reporter covered his ears as the sheep bleated pitifully and writhed in agony. It endured the flames until smoke poured from its mouth, then fell limp.

After the grotesque sacrifice and ceremony, Juvenal and the children – or the 'Prometheans' as he called them – went indoors, where a sumptuous banquet had been prepared. Seated next to Juvenal at the table during the feast, Robinson quizzed him about his presence at various fires in the city. By way of explanation, Juvenal said that he was a practising occultist, who experienced premonitions about the places where fires would take lives. Armed with this foreknowledge of the blazes, Juvenal was able to arrive in time to see them break out. He insisted that he had never resorted to blatant arson.

He then rambled on about the ancient Celtic feast of Samhain and the obscure rituals involving burning effigies of Judas which the Lancashire authorities were clamping down on, and of the late Dr William Price, the father of human cremation. Juvenal agreed with Price on the subject of burial, arguing that it was the antithesis of all that was aesthetic, hygienic, and scientific, and that it caused vast wastage of land and pollution.

"Sooner or later we will run out of cemetery land and we

will have to either burn the dead or recycle them," Juvenal told Robinson.

Alfred Robinson doubted if his editor would ever publish these rantings of a madman, but scribbled furiously nevertheless in his shorthand note book, recording everything that was said to him.

"At midnight I will show you something very spectacular," Juvenal promised.

"What would that be, sir?"

"If your nerves can take it, I shall show you the tortured souls of Hell," replied Juvenal calmly.

At nine o'clock sharp, Juvenal and the Prometheans divested themselves of their ceremonial hats and robes. Juvenal then donned his silk top hat, a black frock coat, and a long, black, satin-lined cape. The children, on the other hand, took up their ragged clothes once more and walked barefoot out of the grand house, but at least their bellies were now full. They were all going to watch another fatal blaze that had been foreseen by their benefactor. Robinson was very sceptical about the whole affair but, sure enough, after walking for almost an hour, the seven of them came upon a blazing cottage near a place called Whiston Cross. A woman at one of the upstairs windows was screaming out for help and in desperation threw her baby, which was cocooned in several blankets, down towards the gawping children. The Prometheans made no effort to catch the baby, but Alfred Robinson leapt forward and just managed to catch the small crying bundle, clutching it to his chest.

"Jump woman!" Juvenal cackled, gazing up at the terror-stricken woman, who was coughing and choking as the smoke poured out of the open window in thick black clouds.

"Jump!" cried the Prometheans in unison.

The woman struggled to get her foot on to the window

ledge in an attempt to climb out of the burning cottage, but as she did so, the flames rose up her long dress and within seconds they had engulfed her. She tried to jump, but as she did so, her dress became snagged on something and she dangled, upside down, just out of reach of any help from below, as the breeze fanned her flaming garments.

The reporter urged Juvenal and the children to help the woman, but they simply laughed and did nothing but avidly observe the unfolding scenario. Robinson was forced to watch impotently as the inverted woman frantically kicked her legs as she burned alive. As soon as the flames had consumed her, the burnt dress gave way and she plummeted to the ground, a smouldering heap which looked barely human.

The burning cottage was in such a remote rural location, that no one came to extinguish the blaze. Juvenal and the children said nothing, their faces betraying no sympathy for either the woman or her orphaned baby. After the fire had died down to the smouldering stage, at a signal from Juvenal, they all returned to their home, the children trooping behind their evil master. The journalist followed, holding the baby and cursing Juvenal under his breath. He felt sickened and confused by the shock of witnessing the woman's horrific death. But worse was still to come.

Back at Juvenal's house, the traumatised journalist suggested that one of the children had been sent to start the fire at the Whiston cottage. This enraged Juvenal and he raised his cane above his head and seemed about to bring it down on the reporter's skull, but stopped at the last moment and stood there trembling instead. He fell backwards and landed in his chair, spitting foam. He eyes fixed on the crying baby in Robinson's lap, and with a sneer suggested that it should be given up to Moloch.

"Over my dead body," said Robinson, through gritted

teeth, clutching the baby even tighter to his chest.

Juvenal smiled and pretended that it had been a jest in bad taste, and offered the reporter a glass of wine.

"This baby needs medical attention," insisted Robinson.

The baby had not stopped crying since the fire and he thought it might have sustained an injury when it landed so heavily in his arms. He stood up and told Juvenal that he was leaving, but the eccentric old man urged him to stay until midnight, which was just half an hour away now. Robinson shook his head and said that he had seen more than enough of the goings on in the Juvenal household. He began to fear for his own life, and headed towards the door. Juvenal pleaded with him, and promised that the manifestations he would conjure up with fire and incantations would terrify but fascinate the readers of the *Chronicle*. The baby had suddenly stopped crying, and was looking placidly at him. The reporter wasn't sure what to do. Should he leave now and take the baby to a hospital, or should he wait a while longer and see what further hocus-pocus the madman was going to stage.

"Very well, Mr Robinson, we shall do it now," said Juvenal.

He stormed off and beckoned to the children to follow. They left the dining hall, and Robinson rocked the baby in front of a blazing fire as he ran through the night's strange events in his mind. Juvenal and the Prometheans returned minutes later, dressed up once again in their outlandish costumes.

"Come, sir, and see the power of eternal fire," said Juvenal.

They went outside and Juvenal lit his own torch and then lit each of the children's torches in turn. He led them to the far end of the vast garden at the rear of the house. A thick wooden beam, about six feet in length, rested on two columns of stones, and between these stones were several bales of hay, covered with brushwood. A white circle had been painted on the grass, and it encompassed the wooden beam and the hay. At various points around this circle, were written many strange words and symbols which held no meaning for Robinson, who had seen too much already and was now determined to leave Juvenal and his little mindless robots at the first opportunity.

Juvenal raised his torch to the sky and recited various phrases in an unknown language, and the children answered several times with equally strange words. Robinson was becoming increasingly restless, and was getting ready to make his escape. The torch which Juvenal held was lowered and thrust at the hay bails. The only welcoming effect was the warmth that bathed Robinson and the swathed baby. The fire quickly rose and the flames licked at the wooden beam, then one of the children suddenly swung a bucket full of inflammable liquid at the beam. It saturated the beam, and in an instant, blue white and yellow flames spat everywhere.

Robinson instinctively shielded the baby from the intense heat, and turned his back on the senseless ritual. Then he heard strange moaning voices. The children gasped in awe, and some of them started to giggle. The reporter half-turned towards the fierce fire and saw something he would never be able to explain or erase from his memory for the rest of his life. A grotesque array of scarlet and yellow faces, all grimacing in terrible agonies, were emerging from the blazing beam. Some let out a stream of filthy swear words and begged for help as their faces became distorted by the flames. Some of the faces were skeletal with rattling jaws, whilst others looked human, but their skin gradually peeled away in blackened layers until only a skull was left. Some of the apparitions had outstretched arms, as if seeking help, and these would slowly melt back into flames.

Juvenal came over and explained what was transpiring to the reporter. "That's not just any old piece of wood, it's the old hanging beam from the gallows at Kirkdale Gaol. I paid a pretty price for it. It has absorbed the souls and minds of so many evil people over the years. Look at them. Watch them suffer."

Just then a strange gale sprang up from nowhere and blasted the fire, showering the children with sparks and glowing embers. Thunder rolled in the skies, and a hard rain started to fall. Alfred Robinson saw his chance, and dashed off, clutching the baby close to him. The sprightly Henry Juvenal immediately gave chase, and Robinson was in no doubt that he was running for his life. The fear of death and the fate of the helpless baby filled the reporter with an adrenalin rush, and he was soon able to outdistance the weird old occultist and his strange brood of tiny servants.

The reporter and the baby survived the incident, but the *London Chronicle* did not print a word of Alfred Robinson's article, because the editor considered that it was in bad taste and would be sure to result in some kind of lawsuit.

Henry Juvenal died and was unofficially cremated, according to his wishes, at Scarth Hill, near Ormskirk, in 1911. The stone idol representing Moloch in his garden was pulled down and broken up by a Presbyterian sect in 1912.

BACK ON TRACK

A calm cold night had fallen on the city of Liverpool. High above the haze of the factory smoke-stacks in the north, a full moon shone down on the night of Tuesday, 24 May 1910. Even the brilliance of the lunar orb was not sufficiently bright to blot out that mysterious ghost from the depths of time and space –

limitless heavens near the constellations of Gemini and Leo. This was the twenty-ninth recorded visit of the great celestial apparition, and in her time she had looked down many times each century to witness the rise and fall of civilisations and the tardy advancement of mankind.

On this occasion, however, the long-tailed comet looked down on a truly pitiful sight; dozens of homeless and discarded mortals, sleeping hunched up under thin sheets of newspaper, in the city's parks. Perhaps a few of these unfortunate souls stirred from their alfresco slumbers and caught a glimpse of the comet before pulling their newspaper blankets over their faces and sinking back into the happier world of dreams. Elsewhere, a policeman strolling on his beat, regularly eyed the unfamiliar smudge of light, and a few of those privileged enough to be sleeping under a roof, took a thoughtful gaze at the comet through their bedroom windows.

Ethel Godwinson, a frail sixty-year-old widow, was amongst this latter group. She gazed at the spectral comet in the western sky and thought about all of the panic it had engendered. She was an avid reader of the newspapers, and had followed every scare-mongering article on Comet Halley. Astronomers had apparently detected poisonous cyanogen gas in the spectrum of its tail and it had been predicted that the Earth would pass through it. Fortunately, the comet's nucleus only passed within thirteen million miles of Earth, yet we did pass through the outer portion of its tail. Luckily for the human race, the cyanogen gas posed no threat to the planet.

Mrs Godwinson dwelt for a while on the unfathomable scale of outer space, the origin of the universe and the meaning of life, before turning in for the night. She was on the brink of sleep when she heard something outside her bedroom door. As she lived alone, it had to be an intruder, and she cowered in her bed. The door creaked open, and the shadowy form of a chubby man entered. She held her breath, but in a heartbeat the fellow was upon her, holding the blade of a clasp knife to her throat.

"You make even a peep and you're dead!" he warned, in a distinctive Northern Irish accent.

Mrs Godwinson's late neighbour, old Mr McKay, had been raised in Belfast, so she recognised it at once. She cried out as the moonlight filtering through the curtains glinted on a knife-wielding hand – a hand with half of its forefinger missing. The other hand pressed down hard on her bosom, and across the knuckles slithered the tattoo of a snake. A handkerchief covered the bottom half of the knifeman's face and his peaked cap cast a shadow over the remaining half. He ordered the terrified widow out of bed and seemed to know all about the small wooden chest hidden under the bed, which contained the five hundred pounds of her life savings. Kicking her viciously in the ribs, he made her drag it out. The thug was soon stuffing the money into his pockets, and Mrs Godwinson felt some relief – at least her ordeal would soon be over now that he had what he wanted. Not a bit of it! The burglar started slapping her hard across the face, and warned her that if she tried to raise the alarm after he had left, he would come back and slit her throat.

The police were not contacted until the next morning, when the bruised and battered widow finally dared to venture out of her bedroom. Not only had the nine-and-a-half fingered thief robbed all her savings, he had also stolen her jewellery from the velvet-lined box in a cabinet in the parlour, including a distinctive gold St Christopher's medal, which had been in her family for generations. Ethel's son Michael swore to track down the blackguard who had reduced his frail mother to a nervous wreck. The police knew of no one in the underworld who matched the man's description, and as the weeks went by, no progress was made by the detectives on the case.

In July of that year, just two months after the robbery, a curious coincidence took place. A priest visited Ethel's Everton home and during a long conversation with her, told of an old superstition associated with St Christopher – the saint featured on the stolen medal. Years ago, in Ireland, when people wanted to find money that had been lost or stolen, they would say, "Saint Christopher, Saint Christopher, return that which is rightly mine!" After which, a reversal of the misfortune would take place, and the missing or stolen items would soon be recovered. This was because Saint Christopher was the patron saint of lost causes and mislaid objects. Mrs Godwinson duly recited the saint's name twice over and asked for her savings and jewellery to be returned. She had little faith that the incantation would work, reciting it more for the sake of the priest than anything else.

This all took place at half-past one in the afternoon. At that precise time, a short overweight man in a cloth cap entered the dark warren of shops and offices at Tuton Chambers on Lime Street, and walked upstairs to a tattooing studio. The man was Rory Kavanagh, and he told the tattooist precisely what he wanted in a raw Northern Irish accent: a naked woman lying stretched out across his back. He pointed to the framed drawing of the woman in question displayed on the wall – with half a forefinger! The tattoo artist – Michael Godwinson – also noted the writhing green serpent tattooed across the knuckles of his other hand. When Kavanagh stripped to the waist, Michael instantly recognised his mother's Saint Christopher medal hanging on a chain from his neck. His customer was the very brute who had robbed and attacked her. Beneath his composed exterior, Michael Godwinson was seething and had to suppress a strong desire to batter the Irishman's head in. Instead of which, he exacted a very unusual revenge upon the robber. Instead of tattooing a naked lady upon Kavanagh's fleshy back, he inscribed, in capital letters, the sentence, 'I AM A THIEF AND A WOMAN BEATER' in a very aesthetic-looking font.

After finishing the last letter, he made an excuse to leave the room and hailed a policeman. Kavanagh was arrested, and although he had already spent some of Mrs Godwinson's life-savings, the rest of the money and most of the jewellery was recovered, along with the loot from some of Kavanagh's other cowardly crimes. Rory Kavanagh was given twelve years' hard labour for his crimes, and for the rest of his life, he carried the tattooed words of shame on his back.

A CHANGE OF FORTUNE

One rainy evening, in September 1862, two women walked down Brownlow Hill towards the towering grimness of the Liverpool Workhouse. They were Margaret Jones, aged seventy, and her thirty-five-year-old daughter, Mary Taylor, the mother of six children. Grey haired, bent and feeble, the widow Maggie Jones hugged her daughter at the workhouse door and surveyed the young woman's careworn face.

"Here, Mary," said Mrs Jones, removing her wedding ring from her bony finger. "Take this."

"No, Mam, I'll not have that!" protested Mary, seizing the ring and placing it back on the finger where it had been proudly worn for over fifty years.

"You could pawn it, my lovely," said Mrs Jones, tears welling in her grey-blue eyes.

"I'll get by somehow, Mam, but certainly not by selling your wedding ring," said Mary, and she too started to cry.

"Oh mother, I don't want you to go into that place, you know I don't," Mary looked with despair at the workhouse door. "Please come back home with me."

"I'd only be a burden on you and Jim. You and he have mouths to feed and Jim's out of work. My health is bad as well. It's not so bad in here, love, they give me medicine," Margaret Jones told her sniffling daughter.

The old lady rang the bell, and a pauper janitor opened the small gate in the main heavy oaken door. Mother and daughter embraced, and then went their separate ways. At least Mary had enjoyed her mother's day out from the abominable workhouse, but the future looked so bleak. Husband Jim was out of work, and her children were walking around barefoot.

When Mary Taylor reached her little home off London Road, she saw Jim and his friend Mick talking in hushed tones by the fireside. As she stoked up the fire, she overheard something that made her heart leap. Jim and Mick were discussing a robbery. As Mary cooked potatoes for the children, Jim came into the kitchen, and told her about the plan. He and Mick intended to rob the house of a rich merchant in south Liverpool the following evening. Mary begged him not to do it, but Jim told her he had to, or they'd all starve. Each day Jim had trudged down to the docks and begged for work, but to no avail, and finding a job elsewhere was well nigh impossible. So it was robbery or the workhouse for Jim Taylor.

That night, in bed, Mary cried bitter tears, and at one point got up and pleaded with God to change her luck. She didn't want her husband to go to prison.

"Please, Lord, I need money so desperately," she whispered. "I don't know where to turn."

That same night, an old man called at the Liverpool

Workhouse with several sacks of potatoes and bags of flour. He said they'd been sent from Hillside Farm in Childwall for the harvest festival at the workhouse. From nine o'clock in the evening until one in the morning, Margaret Jones was told to peel the potatoes in three of the sacks with another old woman. This task was completed, and on the following morning, Mrs Jones asked to see her daughter, and a priest who knew the family visited Mary Taylor and told her to go to the workhouse. Mrs Jones hugged her daughter when she saw her, then told her about a strange occurrence.

At midnight, her hands red and sore from hours of peeling, she had picked up yet another of the potatoes to peel, and found it to be as heavy as a stone. She inserted the knife, which hit something hard in the centre of the potato. Curious to find out what it was, she cut the potato in half and prised out a large nugget of what seemed to be gold. She washed it under the tap and it shone brilliantly, so she slipped it into her apron pocket and carried on with her work, hardly able to contain her excitement. What if it really was gold? She would be able to leave the workhouse and take care of Mary and her family.

Mary took the four-inch long nugget to a trustworthy jeweller – it was the real thing, and weighed nine Troy ounces. It was exceptionally pure and worth over a thousand pounds. Margaret gave the nugget to her poverty-stricken daughter and it changed all their lives. Jim Taylor didn't have to burgle the house in Aigburth and their future was secured.

When the Childwall farmer was told about the gold that had been found in one of his potatoes, he looked puzzled and insisted that he had sent no food for any harvest festival. The old man who had delivered the potatoes to the workhouse was never seen again, and Mrs Jones and her daughter Mary were convinced that he had been an angel of mercy.